THE
SECOND SUPER

LOGAN
RUTHERFORD

CHAPTER 1

THE INTERVIEW

September 19th, 2078

LEOPOLD RENNER BARELY registered the sound of his car's autopilot telling him he'd arrived at his destination. He was distracted by the possibilities of what he was about to learn, so it wasn't until the friendly female voice told him a second time that he'd arrived at the Tempest Memorial Museum that it finally registered with him.

"Thank you," he mumbled as reached over to his driver's seat to grab his tablet.

Leopold climbed out of his dark blue car and closed the door behind him. The car drove off on its own, going to find a parking space. Leopold wished it hadn't gone so fast. He wanted to look at his reflection in the car's smooth skin to make sure he looked nice. However, he would've found nothing wrong. He would've seen that each curl of his brown hair was placed perfectly, just like it was every day thanks to his genetically modified follicles. He would've seen that his green eyes were piercing as always, and that his early-thirties face looked not a day over twenty.

Still, despite looking so meticulous, Leopold felt as if he should've brushed his teeth himself instead of using his personal hygiene robot, just to be sure everything was perfect.

He walked up the steps to the museum, which was an old white house that was taller than it was wide. Leopold walked across the porch, the creaking boards beneath him giving him an uneasy feeling. He wasn't used to sounds like that. Sound of age and strain.

He knocked on the dark green door and waited. While he waited, he checked around, looking for signs of anyone else. He found it strange that the place wasn't bustling with activity. This was, after all, the Tempest Memorial Museum. The news had just broken recently that the museum curator was in fact the widow of Tempest, who she said was a man by the name of Kane Andrews. Leopold, being one of the top reporters in the country, had packed up his vehicle and sped to the museum as fast as he could. So the fact that there was no one else there before him, Leopold found peculiar.

The door opened, and bells jingled from within the museum. Standing on the other side of the door stood the museum curator, Mrs. Andrews. She looked up at Leopold with sparkling eyes and a smile that was as bright as it was warm. Wrinkles shifted and spread across her face, a rarity in a world where people could live to be almost a hundred and fifty before wrinkles even began to show. "You must be Mr. Renner," she said as she looked Leopold up and down, her stark white ponytail bouncing around with the movement of her head.

Leopold gave her a genuine smile and reached out his hand. "Yes, ma'am," he said as he shook her frail hand. "And you must be Mrs. Andrews."

At the mention of her name, Mrs. Andrews smiled even bigger and her eyes brightened even more. "You betcha," she said with a wink.

Leopold already adored the woman's charisma, and his excitement grew that much more.

Mrs. Andrews stood to the side, gesturing for Leopold to come in. "Come on in, Mr. Renner. What'll it be, tea or coffee?"

"Coffee," Leopold said as he walked into the foyer. His mouth hung open from the last syllable, though. He couldn't find the strength or will to close it as he looked upon the headgear of his hero. *The* hero.

Tempest's crimson headpiece with navy stitching around the eyes sat on a bust underneath a glass case.

"Where's the rest of it?" Leopold asked.

"That's a question I can't answer," Mrs. Andrews said with a sly smile.

She disappeared through a door, which Leopold assumed led to the kitchen. He gazed around the room for a moment, looking at all the things in the cases. A piece of steel girder from Tempest's and Richter's first real battle, a duplicate of a sealed Scroll of Power from the Vespa War, a bronze serpent's head from a terrorist organization that had taken Tempest years to bring down… Leopold was overwhelmed by it all.

"This way, Mr. Renner," Mrs. Andrews said from behind him.

Leopold turned around and followed Mrs. Andrews—who held a tray with a mug and a teacup on it—through a set of French doors. She led Leopold to a library that housed tons of books, most of them about Tempest or the other Supers that had come in his wake—both good and evil. Or worse, a chaotic neutral.

Mrs. Andrews set the tray down, then sat herself down in a faded blue recliner. "Have a seat, Mr. Renner," she said as she took the teabag out of her cup.

Leopold crossed the room, noting the musty book smell in his head, and in turn it appeared written down on the screen of the tablet he held in his hands. He sat down on the faded blue love seat that matched the recliner Mrs. Andrews was sitting in.

"Will you be using that tablet?" she asked as nicely as she could, but Leopold could still hear a hint of a condescending tone.

"Yes, ma'am. Is that all right with you?" Leopold asked, not wanting to offend her.

"Yes, of course. Whatever it takes," she said as she put down her teacup. "But in case you couldn't tell, I have a liking for the archaic," she added with a discreet chuckle, as if she'd just shared an inside joke with a friend.

"Well, using a tablet is considered archaic by some people's standards," Leopold said, trying his best to be in on the joke.

Mrs. Andrews gave an innocent laugh and nodded. "Yes, of course."

Leopold reached for his coffee and took a sip. "So," he began as he set down his mug, "Mrs. Andrews. I guess the question that I think is on a lot of people's minds is simple: Why?"

Mrs. Andrews burst out laughing. "Oh, my, Mr. Renner. That is a simple question, yet very complicated. Could you be a bit more specific?"

Leopold sat for a moment, thinking. There were so many

questions he wanted to ask, he didn't know where to begin. He was hoping Mrs. Andrews would just start going and he could just be a note-taker, relishing the information he was being given. He wiped his clammy hands on his khaki pants and thought of his second question. "Why is there no one else here?"

Mrs. Andrews's smile turned sad. "Because most people have forgotten. My husband is now a mere memory in most people's minds. A legend. He and the other Supers brought humanity into a new age, but they all died off along with the times."

It made sense to Leopold. He only knew so much about Tempest and the other Supers because of what they'd done for him personally. Studying them was a bit of an obsession for him. Time moved so quickly nowadays, and people's attention spans were notoriously short. They didn't care about the Supers of the past, and after the events that had led to the end of the Super era, most were eager to forget.

"Why did you just now come forward with Tempest's identity?" Leopold asked next.

Mrs. Andrews sat for a moment, staring into her tea as if the dark liquid held the answer to his question. "Because," she began. "I miss him." She looked up at Leopold with watery eyes. "And he deserves for people to know who he was. How great he was. I don't have much time left on this Earth," she said, examining her frail, wrinkled arms. "I've stayed away from anything that would extend my life. Those things would just prolong my time away from Kane, who's waiting for me up above." Her face brightened up. Leopold could only imagine she was thinking about seeing him again, which struck a sad chord within him. "I'm the only one left who knows the story of Kane Andrews. And it's about time that story was told."

Now it was Leopold's turn to smile as big as he could. "Well," he said, doing his best to contain his childish glee. "I'm ready to listen."

Mrs. Andrews nodded. "Well, then, Mr. Renner, let's begin."

CHAPTER 2

BROKEN WINDOWS

July 7th, 2015

I SAT ON THE couch in my ranch house in Indiana, watching the television as the person referred to as Richter went on his rampage through New York City.

"The eighteen-year-old Patrick Henry—referred to as Richter—is continuing his seventh rampage in New York City," the newscaster said in a voiceover of the shaky footage that showed Richter standing in the middle of the road, picking up cars and throwing them to see how far they could go. He was acting like a kid in a candy store.

I watched as each car flew farther and farther, going until they were tiny dots in the distance.

"Kane, turn that off," my mom said from the front door entryway next to the living room. "I don't want to see anybody getting killed."

"He's not going to kill anybody, Mom," I said. "The city's evacuated. He's just dicking around."

"Turn it off, and watch your language," she said, her fiery

red hair matching the tone of her voice. She walked out of the room, and I continued watching the news.

On one hand, the fact that I was watching someone with superpowers was cool. On the other, the newscaster's monologue was reminding me why Richter had the entire world in a state of fear and panic.

"All attempts to subdue Richter have been met with failure. The number of lives lost totals in the tens of thousands, and those missing easily top that. We are witnessing someone barely out of high school turning the world into his playground, having no regard for the safety and lives of others."

My stomach twisted. I couldn't even imagine what Richter's appearance meant for the future. If no one could bring him down, I didn't even want to think about how many lives would be lost. All I knew was that for the immediate future, the Earth was in gridlock. Always watching for any sign of Richter and the destruction that would follow.

"We are getting reports of two high-speed bogeys heading toward Richter's location. We are getting confirmation that the United States military is launching missiles at Richter. I repeat, missiles launched at New York City, in an attempt to stop Richter."

My attention turned from my thoughts and back to the television screen. As one of the missiles neared, Richter picked up a green SUV and threw it at the missile. The car and the missile both exploded on impact, just a few hundred feet from where the guerrilla-style cameramen were positioned, sending them flying backwards.

The camera flipped and rolled, sending images of a burning New York City rolling across the televisions, phones, and computer screens of billions around the globe. The camera settled on a shot of Richter, right before the second missile reached him. He flew toward it, meeting it in the air. He grabbed hold of it and sent it flying into a building down the street, causing a massive explosion.

The camera moved as the cameraman regained his composure and went back to filming.

Richter's glowing blue eyes turned straight toward the lens of the camera, looking into the eyes of billions. His brown hair blew in the wind, and he raised his hands as if challenging all those watching. He lowered his hands and jumped into the air, and flew toward the building right behind the cameraman. A sonic boom erupted as he slammed into the building faster than the speed of sound.

The cameraman pointed his camera up, trying to follow Richter, but all the camera could capture was the building beginning to crumble as it collapsed on top of the cameraman.

The feed went black and cut back to the shocked faces of the reporters in the newsroom. I glanced away from the television, looking outside. I regretted not listening to Mom and not turning off the television sooner. My stomach turned, fear gripping it. But then something even more terrifying happened, drilling home the fact that nowhere was safe.

Richter himself flew past the windows of my two-story ranch house at such a high speed that the windows shattered, and I was thrown to the floor.

Mom let out a scream. "Are you okay?" she shouted. She ran into the living room, came to my side and helped me up.

"Yeah, I'm good," I said.

"What was that?" She turned and looked out the window, trying to piece together what had happened.

"It was Richter," I said.

My mother's face turned white. She wasn't able to say anything, she was so shocked.

"Don't worry, he's probably somewhere in California by now," I said, answering one of the questions I knew she was going to ask.

"You mean he got from New York to Indiana in *seconds?*"

I nodded.

"Holy shit," she cursed, which was something she almost never did around me, even though I was a senior in high school and heard things ten times worse every day at school.

The front door to the house burst open and Dad came running in. "What's going on? Are you alright?" he said, running over to me.

"Yeah, Dad, we're fine," I said. "Richter flew by so fast he shattered the windows."

My father ran his fingers through his thick brown hair and then rubbed his deep blue eyes. "This is some B.S.," he muttered.

"It'll be alright, Andy," Mom said in a sweet voice as she placed her arm around her husband's waist. Even though she tried to shrug it off, worry still hung heavy on her face.

Dad sighed again, examining the damage with his tired eyes. "When we moved out here I worried about some punk teenagers messing with us because we were so far out, away from the police. I never thought that punk teenager would have superpowers."

That got a chuckle out of me, which in turn caused Mom and Dad to begin laughing too. It was so ridiculous that laughing was the only thing we could do. We began to clean up the windows, still chuckling from the shock that our windows had been blown out by a supervillain.

I FINISHED SENDING A text to my best friend, Drew, as I walked down the stairs. I ruffled my fingers through my curly brown hair, giving it the messy look that I loved.

"Going somewhere?" Mom asked, based on the way I was walking with purpose.

"Yeah," I said. "I gotta go to the shelter. I'm meeting Drew there, and we're gonna help out for a few hours."

Mom dabbed at the sweat beading on her forehead. "Maybe this summer heat is getting to me, but it sounds like you just said you were going out?"

I rolled my eyes. "Yes, Mom, I am. I'll be fine. Richter is probably on the other side of the world by now."

She pursed her lips and shook her head with disapproval. "Still, I don't like it. I'd rather you be safe at home."

"Yeah, you're right, this house is Richter-proof. I forgot," I said as I made my way to the front door. "And this house wouldn't be so hot if you weren't so anti-AC!" I said over my shoulder with a teasing smile.

"Air conditioning costs money!" Mom shot back. "And

now there's a nice breeze, thanks to Richter," she said, motioning to the broken windows.

I chuckled and went outside. I began walking down the sidewalk, but as I walked past the broken windows, Mom stopped me once again.

"Kane," she said to me from inside. "Just be safe, okay?"

I nodded. "Don't worry, Mom, alright?"

She nodded her head and I walked to my car. I climbed into my mid-00's four-door sedan and began the fifteen-minute drive to town.

*

I pulled into the parking lot of Ebon High School and walked to the gym. The front of the lot was full, which meant I had to park in the back. I had a long, hot walk ahead of me. The weather had been hotter than usual as of late, which had led to lots of theories about the correlation between the heat and Richter. Most of them were stupid, like his hideout was in the Sun, which explained both why nobody was able to find him and that he was somehow heating up the Sun. The others were just as ridiculous. However, I guess it could've been true. I mean, no one had tried looking in the Sun, so it could've very well been possible. I highly doubted it, though.

I thought that once I reached the end of my junior year, which had happened just a few weeks ago, I wouldn't have to step foot in my high school until the beginning of my senior year. However, thanks to Richter, my summer plans were drastically altered. The gymnasium of the high school had been turned into a shelter for those who had taken too long to evacuate the cities. The hotel rooms had filled up fast, so shelters like ours were the only option. A couple hundred terrified people crammed into a high school gym made for some interesting experiences, that's for sure. It allowed me to meet a lot of interesting people, however, so even though it kinda smelled and most of the people had bad attitudes, it was fun.

"Hey, man, you ready to enter the lions' den?" somebody asked as they came walking up next to me.

I recognized the voice as soon as I heard it. It was that of my best friend, Drew Polar.

"Lions' den?" I asked as I gave him a fist bump. The two of us walked side by side up the sidewalk, the heat of the Indiana summer sun bearing down on us.

"Yeah," he said. "You didn't see the group text?"

I shook my head as I reached into my pocket to pull out my phone. Displayed on the screen were a dozen group texts between Drew and my other best friend, Michael Teller. I skimmed them, but Drew continued talking, filling me in on the details.

"Yeah, apparently Brian Turner was talking to Macy—"

My blood immediately began boiling.

"And she told him to leave her alone because she had a headache and wanted to go take a nap. He did, but five minutes later came to her spot and tried talking to her again—while she was lying down trying to sleep!"

"Holy shit!" I exclaimed. "What an asshole!"

"I know!" Drew agreed.

We reached the gymnasium doors and pushed them open, blasted by cool air. Our ears were assaulted by the cacophony of voices. It was getting close to dinnertime, so most people were inside, instead of congregating outside as usual. That meant the place also reeked of body odor and was hotter than normal, thanks to all the body heat.

"So how is this like the lions' den?" I almost had to shout to be heard. I was nervous about Drew's answer.

"Well, you know Brian's best friend, Tommy?"

I nodded.

"Well, he told Brian about how Macy's been hanging out with Michael and us, and since Brian's hated you since you were still in your mother's womb, he naturally assumes that you and Macy have a thing going on."

"But we do," I said as we walked behind the concession stand that now held the night's dinner instead of the usual candies and hot dogs it did during basketball season.

"Somebody forgot to tell Macy that," Drew teased as he put on his apron.

I put mine on and rolled my eyes. "You said yourself that she told Michael that she thought I was cute."

"Yeah, but so does your grandma, and that doesn't mean anything." Drew grabbed a plate and dumped the night's meal onto it, which consisted of mac and cheese, green beans, and some chicken nuggets.

"You know what I mean, though," I told him as I grabbed a plate of my own and began doing the same. We loaded up our plates and put them on the counter where a hungry refugee would come and grab one.

The concession stand was filled with people, and Drew and I had to practically elbow our way back to the end of the line to begin filling up another plate.

"That's not even the issue here, though. The issue is that Brian wants you out of the picture."

"Brian's always wanted me out of the picture. I can take him if I need to."

Drew laughed and rolled his eyes but didn't say anything more.

I felt like I could take Brian if I needed to, but you can take almost anyone of any size down with a swift kick to the nuts. If we're talking a "fair" fight, though, Brian would have me whupped. I'm not that scrawny; I try to run at least every other day and hit the weights every once in a while. But I'm definitely not buff by any stretch of the imagination. Brian's not all that buff, either. He's got maybe fifteen pounds on me, but he also has years of martial arts experience. Like, this dude could break my arms with his eyes.

I wasn't worried, though. Brian had a lot of talk, but since his father was the deputy sheriff, it was mostly just that. Talk. He'd never actually do anything, unless he wanted his dad to come down on him. And rumor had it that his father showed him no preferential treatment, which seemed like the truth given the black eye Brian showed up to school with every once in a while.

Once Drew and I were finished making plates of food for others, we made two of our own. We walked out onto the crowded gymnasium floor and scanned the sea of cots for Macy. Her wavy red hair stood out in the crowd, and her bright green eyes met my own, sending waves of happiness shooting through me. We made our way down the line of cots and sat down on the ground next to hers.

"Hi," she said with a charming smile.

"Hey," Drew said as he dug into his mac and cheese.

"Hi," I said. I fumbled with my fork and dropped it on the ground. Macy giggled, making me even more self-conscious. "I gotta go grab another one. I'll be right back."

I stood up, and so did Macy. "I'll go with you," she told me.

My heart skipped a beat and I nodded my head. "Alright, cool." *Really? 'Alright, cool' is the best you could come up with?* I thought. When we were in a group, I was relatively normal around Macy. But on the rare occasion when it was just the two of us, I always did something embarrassing. Even though we were in a room filled with hundreds of people and not technically alone, I could feel my make-a-fool-of-yourself engine revving up.

"How was your day, Kane?" Macy asked as we wove through the cots.

"Good, I guess. Oh, shit," I said, suddenly remembering the day's earlier events. "I forgot to tell Drew! Richter flew by my house and shattered all my windows."

Macy stopped walking, and people around us turned and looked at me.

"I-uh-I…" I stumbled over my words. I motioned for Macy to follow and kept walking.

Macy got close enough that I could feel the heat of her breath on my skin. I did my best to ignore it, trying to focus on not doing something foolish. "Are you serious?" she whispered.

I nodded. "I mean, it doesn't mean anything. Just that we were in his path. Crazy, huh?"

Macy scoffed. "Yeah, crazy's one word for it."

I shrugged. "I'm mostly upset that he messed up all of our windows. It's gonna be a pain putting them back up."

Macy placed a hand on my arm and stopped walking. I did as well, my blood pressure going through the roof. "I'm glad you're okay."

I smiled. "Me too."

Macy chuckled and so did I.

Feeling confident, I decided to keep the jokes going. "Hey, I'm perfectly content with only seeing Richter on a television screen." Shit. That wasn't a joke at all!

"I am too," Macy said.

We reached the concession stand and I grabbed my fork. We turned around and headed back to the cots, totally unaware of how ironic the conversation Macy and I had just had would be in a few short days.

CHAPTER 4

GENESIS

I RETURNED HOME AS my father was making his walk
back from the barn to the house, having just finished feed-
ing the livestock. He wiped his arms on his muscular body and
threw a smile my way.

"Hey," I said as I closed my car door and started walking
to the house.

"How was it?" he asked in a teasing voice, and I instantly
knew he was talking about my time with Macy in particular.

My dad was only in his early forties, still young and with
his best years ahead of him. He definitely didn't look like
the farming type, that's for sure. When I was six, we moved
from Indianapolis, where Dad had been a lawyer and Mom
a teacher, to take over the family farm after my grandfather
died. At first Dad was hesitant, but he fell in love with the
farming life fast and swore he'd never go back to the city. Still,
he looked out of place on a farm. He still carried himself like
the corporate lawyer he had been, always making sure his hair
was cut and his beard was trimmed.

"It was good, I guess," I said.

Dad chuckled. "You guess?" He shook his head as if to say, *Ahhh, teenagers.*

"Yeah." We walked into the house and began taking off our shoes. "I mean, she's not going to stay here forever. Eventually, she and her sister will have to move back up to Indy, and I'll probably never see her again."

"Not with that attitude, you won't," Dad said with a smile.

I rolled my eyes and walked through the living room to the stairs. "I'm going upstairs," I announced as I made my way up. "Goodnight, guys!"

Mom and Dad echoed their goodnights, and I got ready for the last few hours of sleep I was going to have before my life changed forever.

*

My mother's screams woke me from sleep. I jumped out of bed, grabbed a pair of sweatpants, and put them on as I scrambled down the hallway.

"Shut up!" The yell of a man's voice I didn't recognize stopped me in my tracks.

We were being robbed.

"Look, we don't have anything valuable. Our livestock is the only thing of worth. Leave my wife alone, and I'll take you to them," my dad said, pleading with the intruders.

"We don't want your dumb cows," a man said. "We want your money, jewelry, anything you got that can make us a pretty dime."

I inched closer to the top of the stairwell and peeked down. There was nobody at the bottom, so if I wanted to see what was going on, I'd have to go halfway down the stairs, as that's where the opening to the first floor began.

"You aren't listening to me," my dad said. "We don't have anything."

"You're telling me that you haven't bought this pretty lady"—my mom began whimpering—"a diamond ring? A pearl necklace?" The intruder's tone was condescending.

I inched down the stairs one by one, being as quiet as possible.

"Yes, that's exactly what I'm telling you," Dad answered.

It wasn't true at all. My mom had more money than she knew what to do with, and there was a safe hidden in the closet containing over twenty grand in cash. The farm wasn't bringing in that kind of money; Dad just had plenty left over from his lawyer days, plus Grandpa had left him a lot of money along with the farm.

But our intruder didn't know that, and Dad wasn't going to tell him if he could help it. He was an ex-lawyer; he'd mastered making people do what he wanted.

I reached the landing halfway down the stairs and peered around the corner. Most of the lights were off, save for the one in the kitchen, which was on the other side of the wide-open living room/den area. There were three intruders in total. One was holding a gun to Mom, another had a knife to Dad's throat, and the one I assumed was the leader stood between the four of them, facing my father.

"You got five seconds to tell me where the most valuable thing in this house is, or else I start searching myself." The intruder whipped out a butterfly knife and walked over to Mom. Her long blonde hair was a mess. She did her best to hold her composure. "Maybe I'll find something valuable here," he said as he pressed the knife flat against Mom's cheek.

She whimpered, but bit her lip to keep from crying out.

Her terror-filled eyes watched the knife blade as it traveled to her neck.

"Or here," the leader said with a smile.

My dad fought against the man holding him back, but the leader pressed the knife deeper into Mom's skin. I watched in horror as she cried out in pain.

"Nah-ah-ah," the leader said, grinning from ear to ear. "Am I getting warmer?" The knife moved down further.

A hand grabbed my shoulder, and I let out a scream. I looked down, and the toothy grin of a large man looked up at me. I was so distracted by Mom, I hadn't even noticed a fourth member of the gang sneaking up on me.

He pulled me down, and I fought against him, kicking and screaming, but my punches did nothing. He was a very large man who laughed at the futility of my struggle.

"Bingo," the leader said, pointing his knife at me.

My dad was going ballistic, but the man restraining him kept his grip, not allowing my dad to escape.

"Be still or I will shoot your wife!" the leader shouted at Dad.

Dad must've believed him, because he stopped fighting.

I, on the other hand, did not. I struggled against the grip of my captor, but he wrapped his arms around me, restraining me. I tried kicking him, but it was no use.

The leader walked over to me and got right up in my face. He was wearing a ski mask, but I could still see his evil eyes, and smell the body odor emanating from his clothes. His breath, however, smelled of baking soda and mint. A stark contrast from the rest of his body, and a smell I became very familiar with as he leaned in close.

"Do you want me to hurt your mommy?" he asked in a babyish voice. "Your daddy?"

I said nothing. I was fuming. Livid. I wanted nothing more than to tear this monster apart. If looks could kill, I would have already killed this dude a thousand times over. My eyes were shooting daggers into his, and I wished they were real.

"You're going to tell me where the money is, aren't you, son?"

The fact that he'd called me "son" made me want to kill him even more.

"Don't do it," my dad told me.

I looked at him, confused. Was all this really worth saving a few thousand dollars?

Police coming, he mouthed.

Relief washed over me. There was hope. Dad must've called them before the intruders got him.

I turned my eyes back to the leader, confidence radiating from me. "Get the hell out of my house," I told him.

The leader let out a bellowing laugh. He leaned back, placing a hand on his chest, laughing as hard as he could. When he leaned back down, however, he brought his knife down deep into my thigh.

I let out a scream as the pain seared through me. My dad shouted in anger and my mom screamed in fear.

Anger swelled within me, and that's when it all began.

I kicked the leader as hard as I could in the chest. He turned into a rag doll and flew across the room, through the kitchen, and slammed into the kitchen sink, causing pipes to break and water to shoot in the air.

I turned my torso and threw the man restraining me to

the right, and he went flying through the air and slammed into the brick wall, then slumped to the ground.

The man who had a gun to Mom began to realize what had just happened, and he pointed the gun toward me. Even though he was on the other side of the room, my instinct was to dive at him, so dive I did. I pushed myself off the ground and cleared the length of the room. I reached out and slammed into the henchman before he even knew what was happening. The two of us fell to the ground hard. I pushed myself up, but the man I had tackled stayed down.

I turned around to get the man who had Dad, but Dad was one step ahead of me. He'd used my distraction to his benefit and had taken his captor down. He was on top of him, punching him over and over again, his hands as much of a bloody mess as his captor's face. Finally Mom pulled him off the man, and the three of us came together in a warm embrace.

Police sirens sounded in the distance. Better late than never.

Cold water reached my feet, and I let out a sharp hiss in surprise. The three of us looked to where the leader of the group was sitting in what was left of our kitchen sink, groaning in pain.

Mom and Dad looked at me with a million questions in their eyes. I knew the answers to none of them.

"I don't know," I said before they could ask. "I just don't know."

CHAPTER 5

THE SECOND SUPER

THE NEXT DAY, Dad and I pulled into the parking lot of the hardware store. There were a lot of things we had to get in order to fix the damage done both by the intruders we'd had last night, and by Richter.

Both Mom and Dad thought it'd be good for us to get right to work on the repairs, in order to take our minds off the events of the day before. Unsurprisingly, I found this very difficult.

Dad and I got out of the car, and we began walking toward the store. The two of us were deep within our own thoughts. Even during the ride to the store, we didn't speak. We were both so confused and scared. Not just by the fact that our lives had been threatened and the safety of our home destroyed, but the way that I'd taken the intruders out.

We'd all come to the conclusion that it was some really intense adrenaline. It made sense. Fight or flight. Like how people are able to lift cars to save loved ones trapped beneath them. If adrenaline could allow someone to lift a car that weighed tons, it'd definitely allow an in-shape seventeen-year-old to kick a hundred-and-seventy-five-pound man across a room, especially when the lives of his family were being threatened.

My phone vibrated in my pocket. I pulled it out as Dad opened the door and I walked into the store. A text from Drew was on the screen; it read:

Dude! You gotta get to the school. There's a news crew here covering the shelter. CAMERAS EVERYWHERE!

I surprised myself when I smiled and chuckled a little.

"What is it?" Dad asked as we walked down one of the plumbing aisles.

I shook my head. "Drew. There's a local station at the high school covering the shelter, and he's freaking out."

Dad shook his head and smiled. "It's a local news station. I don't get what he's freaking out about."

"Because it's Drew, and he finds a way to get excited and freak out about everything."

"I guess that's not a bad way of looking at life." Dad stopped in the aisle and turned to look at the water faucets. "You wanna run up there real quick when we're done here?" he asked as he searched for a faucet he thought would satisfy Mom.

I nodded. "Yeah, that'd be cool. It'd be nice to see Drew and them, plus tell them what went on last night. Wouldn't want them to find out through a newspaper or something."

Dad snapped a picture of a faucet with his phone and sent it to Mom for approval. "Alright, sounds good," he said as we stood there waiting. "I could use the distraction."

I wanted to say "me too," but the words didn't come out. I just grunted and nodded my head. I looked to the ground, trying to contain my excitement at the idea of a distraction.

Mom approved the faucet, and after another hour or so

of shopping, we were loaded up in the car, on our way to the high school.

When we pulled up, we noticed that for some reason everybody—including the news crew—was looking up.

"What in the world?" Dad asked as he parked the car and the two of us got out.

We followed everyone's gaze to see what was going on, and when we saw, I couldn't believe my eyes.

Hovering ten feet above Ebon High School was Richter, his blue eyes glowing bright in the early afternoon sun.

I opened my mouth to say something, but no words came out. Everybody in the parking lot, including Dad and I, stood in awe of him. The sensible thing to do would be to turn and run away, but nobody had it in them. It wasn't like we'd be able to get away, anyway, so we just stood there, terrified, trying to figure out whether he'd show mercy on us or not.

He didn't.

Without saying a word, he floated down to the edge of the rooftop, and from behind the half-wall that surrounded the edge of the roof, he pulled a young woman up by the back of her neck. She screamed in terror as Richter floated into the air and hovered over the edge of the high school, dangling the woman four stories in the air.

"Somebody help, please!" she screamed. I might not have been able to recognize her from afar, but that voice combined with the red hair left no doubt in my mind.

Richter was holding Macy in his clutches, and was about to drop her to her death.

My stomach twisted and heat flushed through my body. I look around, frantic for something—anything—to help her. But I was helpless.

The feeling in my gut grew stronger, and I felt a small vibration reverberate through the ground.

"Kane," my dad said in a quiet voice. It sounded like he was going to say more, so I turned to look at him. Besides myself, he was the only person not looking at Richter and Macy. Instead, he was looking at the gravel floating inches above the ground around my feet.

Startled, I jumped back and the rocks fell to the ground. The vibrations stopped, and I met eyes with my dad, neither of us believing what we'd just seen.

A high-pitched scream pierced the air as everybody gasped in horror. I turned to look, and I screamed in horror too as I saw Macy falling toward the ground.

Craters appeared in the ground as, without even thinking about it, I launched myself into the air toward Macy's falling body. My heart fell to my feet. I felt terrified, with no idea what was going on.

I flew above the crowd of people whose eyes were still fixed on Macy and Richter. I reached Macy in seconds and wrapped my arms around her. I didn't know how, but I slowed the two of us down and floated to the ground.

I looked at Macy, who had passed out in my arms, then looked around for somewhere to put her and realized that every single person in the parking lot was staring at me. Cameras were broadcasting my image to millions—possibly billions—around the world. I could see reflected in the lenses that my eyes were shining a bright, bright white, obscuring my identity from the world.

The sound of my shoes scraping the gravel broke the pin-drop quiet as I walked over to a lady in her early thirties. She looked at me, her eyes filled with terror and confusion. It was a look I imagined everyone would see in my own eyes, if they could see them at all.

I held Macy's unconscious body out to her, but the lady just stared at me, paralyzed with confusion. Not wanting to speak, so as to not give away my identity, I held out Macy a little further, indicating that I wanted the lady to take her.

She held out both her arms, realizing what I was asking of her, and I gently placed Macy across them.

I turned my attention back toward Richter, who was still floating in the air. Even though his eyes were glowing a bright blue, I could still tell by the look on his face that he was as shocked and confused as I—and everyone else watching—was.

Deep craters formed and a deafening boom sounded as I shot through the air, aiming directly for Richter. The world around me seemed to slow as I flew closer to him, and the thought that no one had ever been as close to Richter as I and lived crossed my mind.

My fist connected with the bottom of his jaw, and a booming sound like a loud crack of thunder echoed in the air. Richter flew upwards through the air from the force of my punch, which should have broken every bone in my body. I reached out to try to grab him and slam him into the ground, but I could only grip the black V-neck he was wearing. The shirt ripped off him like it was made of nothing. Richter regained his composure and took one good look at me before turning around and flying off as fast as he could, leaving nothing but a sonic boom in his wake.

I looked down and saw that everyone was still looking at me. There was nothing but complete silence as they all stared, trying to process what they had just seen. My mind was trying to process it as well, but I wouldn't let it. I had all the world's attention, including Richter's, and I needed to send a message before I even tried thinking about what the hell was going on.

I floated over to the edge of the high school and stood on the roof, thankful for my feet to be on something solid.

Then one person started clapping. Then another. And another.

Soon, the crowd of hundreds of people began clapping, shouting—*cheering*—for me. The sound was deafening.

I lifted the hand that held Richter's shirt into the air above my head, and that was when the crowd really went nuts. They were going crazy, screaming at the top of their lungs, jumping up and down in joy. They finally had hope once again.

I pumped the shirt up and down in the air and shouted myself. I looked across the crowd, and my glowing eyes met with my father's. His mouth was wide open in shock, but when he saw I was looking at him, he smiled. He gave me a thumbs-up, and my heart soared.

I looked back across the crowd and began floating in the air once again. They were still going wild as I floated closer to the ground. I looked directly into the news camera and smiled. Then I flew through the air, away from the crowd, shouting and whooping for joy, the crowd still cheering in the background.

Richter was no longer the only superhuman on Earth. There was now a second superhuman, and I couldn't get over the fact that the second Super was me.

CHAPTER 6

THE AFTERMATH

SO MUCH ADRENALINE flowed through my body that I couldn't sit down. I paced across the living room floor, feeling lightheaded and as if I was going to throw up.

Mom was sitting on the couch, her elbows on her knees and her hands on her face. She stared at the wooden floor, searching it as if the reason for my sudden development of superpowers was somehow hidden in the cracks between the planks. Dad was standing close to the television, watching the news report that contained the same footage that was showing on every channel.

"Bystanders watched in horror as Richter dropped seventeen-year-old Macy Westling over four stories at Ebon High School in Ebon, Indiana," news reporter Jane Tanner said, her red lips quivering in excitement. "That is, until another superhuman appeared out of nowhere and caught her."

The footage showed me flying out of nowhere, catching Macy, slowing our descent, and touching down on the ground. Even though I was standing in my living room, terrified, I still couldn't help but feel my heart skip with excitement as I watched what happened next in the footage for the hundredth time.

I turned from handing off Macy and shot off screen. I hadn't even realized how fast I was going until I saw the footage. The cameraman was unable to keep up with me, and by the time he zoomed out and got me back in frame, Richter was flying through the air, righting himself, and giving me one last look before flying off.

"Who is this new superhuman, and will he bring us the same troubles as Richter?" the news reporter asked. "To help answer that question, we have joining us Tom Lance, former head of Homeland Security, and Roland Peterson, host of the number one talk show across America and self-proclaimed 'superhuman expert.' Gentlemen," the reporter said, giving a slight nod as the two video streams appeared on either side of her head.

Even though they were going to say the same things I'd heard them say all night, I stopped pacing and gave the television my full attention.

"Let's start with you, Tom," Jane began. "You're saying that this complicates things more than helps. How so?"

Tom, a man in his sixties, cleared his throat, the loose skin beneath it shaking back and forth as he did so. "Now," he said, "first of all, I'm not saying that this new development isn't good at all. Clearly that's not the case; just ask Ms. Westling. However, it does complicate things a whole lot more. What are we going to do, let this new Super and Richter turn the world into their battlefield?"

"Tom," Roland interrupted, "the world is already Richter's playground. At least if it's a battlefield, that means there's a chance of us winning!"

Tom nodded. "Yes, that's possible; however, we don't know if this new Super is even capable of defeating Richter. And even if he is, who's to say that he won't become the next Richter, huh?"

"Regardless of what this new Super is going to be, *we* are going to all be dead if nobody stops Richter. Right now some guy in Indiana is more capable of doing that than all the world's militaries, and so I'm going to side with that dude. The only person, I might add, who has ever been able to get close to Richter and survive, much less deal an amazingly powerful uppercut that sent Richter packing."

I smirked at that part, but did my best to contain a chuckle. Mom and Dad were freaking out, so if they saw I wasn't taking this as seriously as they were, they might get a little upset. But I was taking it as seriously—no, *more* seriously than they were. I mean, it was me who was on every television, phone, and computer screen around the world. I was the most popular person on the planet at the moment, and the second most-sought-after one, second only to Richter himself. The attention I was receiving alone terrified me, let alone not knowing what was actually going on inside my body. I wasn't totally afraid I was going to die; Richter seemed to be just fine. Still, there was a chance that if my body went on doing whatever the hell it was doing, it would eventually explode or something. Plus, I had no idea how I was going to use my powers, both literally and figuratively. Or whether or not by being around me, my parents would get some sort of radiation poisoning, or something like that, and die.

There were so many unknowns, yet everyone had an idea that they knew exactly what was going to happen next. I would be a knight in shining armor, come to the aid of the world, and defeat Richter, restoring peace and order. Me, on the other hand,… I had a feeling I'd just gotten lucky and had caught Richter off guard. I had no idea how I was going to take him on again.

Still, despite all of that, I couldn't help but try not to laugh every time I heard someone mention my "killer uppercut."

*

Mom, Dad, and I sat around the dinner table, picking at our food. We were all processing what was happening. All I could think about was the things that had happened to Richter's family after the world found out his identity.

As is obvious to most, Richter was always very open about his powers, even from the very beginning. He had no problem with letting people know who he was, because he thought he was invincible. And he was, until I came along. The one thing he didn't take into account was his family.

Family members and friends of some people Richter had killed during his escapades decided to take revenge on Richter and hurt him the same way he had hurt them. They found his parents and younger sister and killed all three of them in their home. Furious, Richter tracked down the people who had killed his family and slaughtered all of them. There weren't even any bodies left intact.

People were terrified of me because they didn't know if I'd be a Richter 2.0. If they knew who I was, they'd act pre-emptively and foolishly. I was terrified that somehow someone would figure out who I was and come find my family. I'd already saved my parents from intruders once, and it wasn't exactly an experience that I wanted to go through again.

"Listen, Kane," my dad said, breaking the silence.

I found it hard to look him in the eye. For some reason, I was terrified of what he might say.

"I think we should lie low for a while. You shouldn't be using any of your..." He searched for the word. "*Abilities*, at least not right now. There's about to be a lot of attention focused on Ebon. We don't know who could be watching."

I nodded. "Yeah, I understand."

"I don't want you going to the shelter, either," Mom said. "Someone might recognize you."

I slumped back in my chair and let out a sigh, obvious in my disappointment.

"Is that really a good idea, Heather?" Dad asked.

"Yeah, Mom," I said. "I just..." I paused, trying to think of the right words to say. "I just think I'd go crazy being locked in the house. I need to see my friends. Try to feel normal, you know? Stay in the loop so I can try to figure out when it's safe for me to start training."

Mom and Dad looked at me, shocked. Mom almost dropped her fork as she let her mouth hang open. "Training?" she exclaimed.

"What do you mean by that?" Dad asked.

I chose my next few words very carefully. "Well, I mean Richter isn't going to stop until everybody on Earth is dead. He's just toying with us right now, having his fun because no one was a threat. Eventually, though, you can bet that pretty much everyone will be dead. But now..." I looked off to the corner of the room, trying to best articulate what I was thinking. "I've complicated things for him. Now there's a threat, and I'm it. I have a feeling he's going to accelerate his plans a little. He's going to be looking for me, and I have to be able to stop him."

Dad stared at his plate of food and nodded. "You're right, Kane. As much as I hate to admit it, you're right."

Mom pursed her lips and shook her head. "I don't like this. I don't like this at all."

"Do I really have a choice?" I asked, looking her in the eye. "People are dying, Mom. I'm the only one who can stop Richter."

"Maybe the government is working on something that can stop him," Mom said, frantic for an answer other than me, her baby, being put in harm's way.

"I doubt it. The government is probably looking for me right now. I'm the only thing that's been proven to work against him."

"You're not a *thing*," Mom said under her breath, her voice quivering. "You're not a thing. Don't ever call yourself a thing."

I sighed. "I'm sorry, Mom. You know what I mean, though."

Mom pushed her plate away and stood up from the table. "I need some fresh air," she said. She walked away from the table and out the front door.

My eyes lingered on the door before I returned my gaze to Dad. He looked at me, his eyes saying so much. He was scared, worried, confused, and whatever other things you feel when you find out your son has superpowers.

"I'm going to go check on your mom," he said as he stood up from the table.

"Okay," I said.

He walked out of the room, and at that moment, I'd never felt more alone.

CHAPTER 7

EXCUSES

I TURNED MY CAR off in the parking lot of the high school. I took a moment and closed my eyes, breathing in and out slowly, trying my best to keep my hands from shaking. I looked up, and my eyes wandered to the police tape around the part of the parking lot I had taken off from. There was a small crater there, a stark reminder of what I'd done. I couldn't help but smile a little. I had to admit it was really freaking cool, although equally terrifying.

I got out of my car and took another deep breath as I made my way into the school. I was scared of what might happen when I got inside. What if someone recognized me? What if *Macy* recognized me? The thought was scary. I didn't know what I'd do.

Speaking of Macy, I was so caught up in my own personal developments that I'd kinda forgotten to be worried about her. However, that came to me in floods as I walked inside the high school, making up for lost time. It'd been a day since the big event, and that definitely wasn't enough time for her to recover. I questioned whether or not she'd even be at school.

I cursed myself for not thinking about that earlier, and began searching the crowd for her signature red hair.

One thing that shocked me as I searched the crowd was how calm everybody was. I was expecting there to be a ton of commotion, unrest, *something.* Instead, everyone was sitting around in silence, a palpable sense of fear lingering in the air. It was the not knowing that scared them the most, I was sure. Not knowing why Richter had come to Ebon—which I myself was wondering—or who I was, and whether or not I was bad. If only they knew that the guy who was on the minds of every person in the world was only a few feet away from them. How would they react?

Alright, stop thinking about that, I told myself. *Find Macy.*

"Kane, what the hell!" I heard Drew whisper to my right.

I turned and saw him walking toward me, with Michael towering by his side. "Hey, guys," I said as I held out my hand and offered a fist bump. They gave me one, but then Drew proceeded to scold me.

"Where have you been?" he all but shouted. "I've been calling, texting, everything! I even sent you an email, for crissakes. *An. Email.* You know what it's like traveling back to 2008? It's not fun."

Michael and I both laughed at Drew. "Sorry, man," I said. "I didn't have a phone signal out on the farm. Besides, I was glued to the television."

"Yeah, me too," Michael said. "I didn't even realize Drew was trying to get hold of me until nine last night."

"I shouldn't have had to!" Drew shouted, flailing his hands in the air. People turned to look at us, and Drew shrank down a bit and whispered. "I shouldn't have had to," he repeated. "Did you not notice a certain redhead being thrown through the air on live television?"

My mind swirled. What was I going to tell Drew? I should've gone and checked on Macy, and I felt bad for not doing so. Still, I was a little distracted. Besides, I was the one who'd saved her, so I was pretty sure she was alright—but nobody else knew that. I'd only had my secret identity for less than twenty-four hours, and already I was about to blow my cover.

"I was out of town at my grandparents'. I didn't get back until this morning. I sent her a text, though," Michael explained.

Drew nodded, satisfied with Michael's answer. He turned to me, and I dreaded every second of what was coming. "What about you, Kane?"

"I just forgot to." *Shit.* That was an awful answer. I mentally gave myself one of my signature uppercuts.

Michael and Drew looked at me with blank faces.

"Well, I mean…" I needed to think of something fast. "I think I can get a free pass on this one, right? I mean, it's been less then forty-eight hours since my house was broken into and my parents were almost killed right before my eyes, so I—"

"WAIT. WHAT THE HELL?!" Drew shouted, eliciting nasty looks from bystanders.

"Alright, start from the beginning right now," Michael said.

I looked at the two of them, confused, before I realized that the whole "becoming a superhuman" thing had happened before I got the chance to tell either of them about the break-in. Yet another thing that had slipped my mind.

I filled the two of them in on the whole story, but when I got to the part where I'd used my superpowers for the first time without even realizing it, I told them that Dad and I had gotten the jump on the intruders. Had I told them that I'd done it myself, they wouldn't have believed me, even if I offered them the adrenaline theory I'd originally believed. They knew me too well.

"Holy shit," Drew breathed once I had finished my story.

"Yeah, bro, seriously, holy shit," Michael agreed. "That's insane. How are you doing? Holding up alright?"

I nodded. "This has been a crazy couple of days. But I really wanna check up on Macy—explain myself and everything."

Drew nodded. "Yeah, of course. She's not staying here anymore, though."

"She and her sister got put up in the Ilan downtown," Michael said. He practically bounced on his feet, he was so excited.

The Ilan was the only five-star hotel we had in Ebon, and it was quite the anomaly. There were a few blocks of office buildings downtown, but nothing huge. Definitely not skyscrapers by any stretch of the imagination. Then there was the Ilan, a tall hotel that towered above the rest. It was like a resort, which was strange, because Ebon was a town of, like, 100,000 tops. There was really no reason why you'd want to go to a resort in the middle of small-town Indiana. Especially not when Indianapolis was nearby. And an airport to take you someplace other than Indiana—because literally anywhere would be a better place to go on a vacation than here.

"Wow, the Ilan. That's pretty cool!" I said.

Drew nodded. "Yeah, for sure. We're about to head to the hospital to help her pack and get her stuff moved over to the hotel."

"Sweet. Let's go," I said.

The three of us turned around and walked out the high school doors, and for some reason, my stomach twisted.

CHAPTER 8

A SURPRISE VISIT

F ROM MACY'S WINDOW, I looked down at the horde of news crews camped in front of the hospital. They were desperate to get any morsel of information from Macy, even though she'd said she didn't remember much, and most of what she did remember was just her fearing for her life. Still, the reporters wanted more. There were multiple guards stationed at her door and at other places around the hospital, as reporters were desperate and would do whatever it took to get a few seconds alone with Macy. If only they knew that both Macy *and* the superhuman who had saved her were standing in the same room together. There was no telling what they'd do to get the scoop on *that* story.

"I'm really sorry about all you had to go through," Macy said from behind me.

I turned from the window to face her. She was sitting up in bed on top of the covers, while Drew and Michael were sitting in two chairs next to the bed. "It's fine," I said as I sat down on the foot of her bed. "Really. You've been through a lot, too."

She grinned and brushed some strands of hair behind her ear. "I guess we can just call it even."

I smiled and nodded. "Yeah, even."

From the corner of my vision I could see Michael elbowing Drew, who was in the middle of an overdramatic eye roll.

"So, when are you getting out?" I asked.

"Well, I could leave today if I wanted. I've had lots of hotels and apartment complexes offer to let me stay there for free for the publicity. The hospital director told me I could stay here until they needed my room, since all the people at the hospital make it a safer place and less of a target."

I tried to hide my wince at hearing her describe herself as a "target." It didn't seem right.

"But Madeline hates staying here, so I think we'll take one of those apartment complexes up on their offer this weekend."

"You're so lucky," Michael said. "Getting a kickass apartment and not having to pay any rent? That's so nice."

Macy nodded. "I'm definitely not complaining."

"I wish you were going to take the Ilan up on their offer like I thought, though. Still, you gotta let us come over and check out your new place," Drew said.

"Of course! Why wouldn't I?"

"Well, you're all big and famous now. We don't want you to forget about us little people, is all," Michael said.

I chuckled, but not at Michael's joke. I was laughing at the fact that one of the most famous people on the planet was sitting right across from him, and he had no idea.

"It's so crazy, though, isn't it?" Michael said.

"You're going to have to be more specific," Drew scoffed. There were way too many crazy things happening to choose from.

"Like… why here, you know? Like, why Ebon of all places? It's crazy."

I zoned out for a moment as I thought about it. I guessed it really was weird that Richter had come to Ebon, of all places, and it happened to be the place where I was living. It all seemed so strange.

Before I could question it further, the door opened, bringing me back to the present. We all turned to see who it was. In walked Madeline, Macy's older sister, the only family she had. She had bags under her dark brown eyes, and her brunette hair was in a messy bun, with strands hanging down around her face. Madeline was twenty-four years old; she worked as a graphic designer in Indianapolis while also taking care of Macy. Not that Macy needed someone to take care of her, but still, Madeline was there to support her when she needed it.

"How are you boys doing?" she asked. She walked over to the table next to the bed and set her purse down on it.

"Men," Drew corrected her with a smile. "And we're doing good."

"Well." This time it was Madeline's turn to correct him. "You're doing well, Michael."

"Actually, I'm Michael," Michael said as he raised his hand. "He's Drew."

"My apologies. All I know for sure is that he's Kane," Madeline said, pointing toward me.

I looked at Macy, whose eyes met mine. She blushed, and she quickly turned her attention to Madeline, shooting her a dirty look.

Madeline gave her a teasing smile, then sat down next to her on the bed. "Oh, there's someone else coming up here.

Another one of your friends. I can't remember his name, but I see him hanging out with you all the time."

I knew exactly who it was, but before I could ask to be certain, the door opened, and in he walked.

It was Brian, the guy who was in love with Macy, who'd hated me my entire life, but even more so now that Macy liked me instead of him. Well, allegedly liked me.

"Hey, Macy," he said. He gave Drew, Michael, and me a disgusted look. "I didn't realize you had company."

"Hello, Brian. Yes, I do. Is there anything I can do for you?" Macy said with a cold tone in her voice.

Brian pulled one of his hands from behind his back and revealed a bouquet of flowers. "I wanted to bring you these, and see how you were doing."

I exchanged a look with Drew and Michael. It was clear we were all taken aback by Brian's uncharacteristically kind gesture, and I wondered what it was he had up his sleeve. Brian always had ulterior motives. He never did something from the kindness of his heart, but always because there was something for him to gain from his actions.

"Can I have a moment?" he asked. He looked at me, anger flashing in his eyes. "Alone."

Macy thought about it for a moment before coming to a decision. "Well, you did bring me some flowers. You can have your moment, but I'd like for my sister to stay in the room, if that's okay with you," she said.

Brian nodded. "Yeah, okay."

Macy turned to us. "This shouldn't take long."

I gave her a look that showed my disapproval, then stood up from my seat on her bed, as did Michael and Drew. We walked to the door, and before I closed it, I turned to Macy. "If you need us, we'll be right outside."

"Alright, I'll keep that in mind." She bit her lip and held back a laugh, causing my heart to skip and a huge smile to break out across my face. Brian stood there, quietly fuming, trying his best to contain his temper.

Drew, Michael, and I stood outside the hospital room, trying to hear what was going on inside. We couldn't get too close, however, since two police officers were standing on either side of the door.

We gave up on eavesdropping and did our best to stay out of the way in the hall, which was easy to do, since it was very wide. A few doctors and nurses walked by occasionally, but for the most part it stayed pretty quiet. Macy was staying in a part of the hospital that wasn't very busy, I guessed because the busy parts were occupied by people who actually needed medical attention.

"So what are you gonna do about your competition?" Drew asked, elbowing me.

I gave him a glare. "Brian isn't competition. He's just being a dick and using her situation for his own gain."

"Maybe so, but still, you gotta admit that the flowers were a nice touch."

"Yeah, Kane," Michael chimed in. "I didn't see you bring her anything."

"Well, it's not like I had the time to or anything," I said, defending myself. *Plus, I'm the one who saved her life, so there's that too,* I thought. *I think that's worth more than a bunch of flowers that'll die in a few days.*

I heard a door behind me open, and I turned around as fast as I could. Brian exited Macy's hospital room and slammed the door behind him. The two police officers went on alert, their hands lingering around their Tasers.

"I'm sorry. I didn't realize how light the door was," Brian said in a rush.

"Either way, the exit's that way, son," one of the officers told Brian. He raised a finger and pointed down the hallway past my group.

"Yeah, alright," Brian mumbled.

His eyes bored into mine the entire time he walked toward us. I stared right back into his, not afraid for a second.

"You're gonna regret thinking you're better than me, Kane," Brian said as he walked by, making sure to stay quiet so the officers wouldn't hear him.

"And you're gonna regret thinking you were good enough for Macy," I spat back at him.

"The hell you say?" he all but shouted at me, stopping in his tracks. His chest was puffed and his arms were flexed, ready for a fight.

"Hey!" one of the officers shouted as they walked over to us. They grabbed Brian by the arms. "Let's go, punk." And with that, they escorted Brian out of the hospital.

I made sure to give him a little wave before he disappeared around the corner. It wouldn't be long until Brian Turner would no longer be a problem.

CHAPTER 9

A HAPPY ACCIDENT

I WALKED OUT OF the Burger Shack, a sack full of food in one hand and a holder of drinks in the other. I walked down the street just a few blocks away from the hospital, breathing in the fresh summer air. I needed to cool down after my confrontation with Brian, so I had volunteered to go get burgers for everybody while the rest of the guys helped Macy pack. The streets were unusually quiet for the summertime in Ebon, but that was becoming more and more the norm thanks to Richter. On the other hand, I walked with a little extra skip in my step, enjoying the beautiful day. I looked forward to seeing Macy again, even though I'd only been away from her for half an hour.

As I passed by a small alleyway just a block away from the hospital, though, my day took a turn for the worse. "Hey, dickhead!" I heard someone call from within the alley. I turned my head to the right to see who it was, and there stood Brian Turner with a face that said he was pissed and ready to raise hell.

I rolled my eyes and sighed. "What is it, Brian?" I asked.

"Come here," he said.

"And why would I do that?" I asked him.

Brian walked toward me, grabbed me by my shirt, and threw me into the alley. The drinks and burgers flew out of my hands, and all over the alley. I hit the ground and rolled a couple of times before stopping face-up, staring at the sky. "Oh, ow!" I shouted, doing a bad job of making it seem like I was in pain, even though I felt nothing at all.

Brian walked over to me and pulled me up by my shirt. He pushed me up against the brick wall on one side of the alley. "You listen to me, and you listen good: stay the hell away from Macy. She's mine, you prick," Brian shouted at me.

"Uh, well, I don't know about that. You can't tell me who I can and can't be friends with, and you also can't tell me who I can and can't be in love with. Especially when that person is in love with me," I said. I didn't know if Macy really was "in love" with me, but I knew that'd sure make Brian mad.

Brian punched me in my gut, and I almost forgot to double over in faux pain.

"She's not in love with you!" Brian shouted. "She loves me, alright? Now, you're going to stay away from her!"

My blood began to boil. Brian had always been a nuisance to me my whole life, and I was tired of it.

He punched me in the stomach again, except this time I did nothing. He didn't seem to notice, though.

"Are you going to leave her alone?" he yelled at me.

I was seething with anger. I couldn't believe the nerve of Brian. He was certifiably insane if he thought that this was how you got a girl.

"No, Brian," I told him, looking him in the eye. "*You're* going to leave her alone."

Brian looked at me, confused. "The hell you say."

"I said," I began, standing up a little straighter. "You're going to leave her alone."

Brian punched me again in my face, which did nothing but make me even angrier. I put both hands on his shoulders and pushed him, sending him flying into the brick wall just a few feet behind him. The wall cracked and caved in a little on impact, and Brian fell in a heap on the ground, unconscious. Blood began to pool around him as I'd realized what I'd done.

"Oh shit," I breathed. "Oh shit, oh shit, oh shit!"

I pulled out my phone and called 911, trying to think of the story I was going to tell the authorities when they reached me.

*

Macy, Drew, Michael, and I each sat in our own corner of the waiting room. We hadn't been sitting there for long, but it'd been a couple of hours since my encounter with Brian in the alleyway. I'd convinced everyone that we should wait for some news in the waiting room. I'd said it was because we had nothing better to do, but really, I just wanted to know he was okay as soon as possible.

"It's such a good thing you walked by when you did," Macy said for probably the millionth time, which annoyed me to no end. I didn't understand why she was so happy Brian was okay. I mean, yeah, I was glad he wasn't dead, but she wouldn't shut up about it.

I shrugged and made an *mmhmm* noise.

"You could've not been, quote, so shocked I dropped the food and drinks I was holding, end quote. This hospital food has nothing on Burger Shack," Drew said, his face twisting in disgust at the mention of the hospital food.

"I'm really sorry about that, guys. I'll buy everybody's food tomorrow," I said.

"Oh, you'd better!" Michael said.

I heard a door open and turned to look, as did everyone else in the waiting room. A nurse walked in and made a beeline for Brian's parents.

The room was big and filled with people, and his parents were across the room, so I couldn't hear what she was saying. I wanted to so badly, though. I strained my ears and leaned forward, wishing as hard as I could that I could hear whether or not he'd be okay. Suddenly, I could hear her voice as clear as day.

"Broken ribs, punctured lungs, and internal bleeding. The doctors are working as hard as they can, and they are very confident that your son will be okay."

Brian's mother burst into tears and hugged the nurse as tight as she could. The nurse smiled and patted her on the back.

I sank back into my chair and smiled, flooded with relief. I felt so good. Brian would be okay, and he wasn't going to mess with me again. Everything was turning out in my favor. Plus I'd found out I had super hearing! I was floating on cloud nine.

"It looks like everything's going to be okay," Michael said as he watched the scene.

I nodded my head. "Yep, Michael. Everything's turning out perfectly."

CHAPTER 10

A TERRIBLE MISTAKE

I WALKED INTO MY house and quietly closed the door behind me. It was late, well past midnight. I began to sneak quietly to my room, but there was a figure sitting on the couch. I stopped in my tracks and turned to face it, but then I saw that it was just my dad.

"Kinda late, huh?" he asked.

I felt my body fill with fear at the trouble I might be in. Not that I'd done anything wrong, since my curfew wasn't until one, but there was something about the way Dad had waited up for me and had spoken to me that had me worried. "Yeah, I guess. Been a long day."

"So I've heard."

A moment of silence passed between us before he continued.

"Kane, I heard about what you did to Brian."

I gulped. "Yeah, well, he'll be okay. I didn't hurt him too bad."

Dad scoffed and raised a hand. "Oh, not too bad. I guess everything's fine, then, huh?"

"What's your point, Dad? Brian was being the bully he's

always been, and I stood up for myself. I don't see what the problem is."

"The problem is that you could've killed Brian, Kane. Parents could be mourning the loss of their son right now, and it would've been your fault."

I thought about it for a moment. I would've felt really guilty had I killed Brian. But still, I hadn't. I didn't see what the huge problem was. "Don't worry, Dad. Everything's going to be okay. It's not like I went after him. He's the one who attacked me. I just defended myself, is all."

Dad sat back in his seat and took a deep breath. "I'm just asking that you please be careful. And pray that Brian doesn't remember much when he wakes up. He may be stupid, but he's not an idiot. If he's able to put two and two together, he'll be able to figure out who you are. You were being careless, son. You let your emotions get the best of you. Just pray that it doesn't come to bite you or anyone else in the ass."

I nodded my head. "Alright. Can I go to bed now?"

Dad nodded. "Goodnight, Kane. I love you."

"You too," I muttered under my breath as I turned around and made my way to my room.

When I got into my room, I didn't even turn the lights on. I just stripped down to my boxers and climbed into bed. I plugged my phone in to charge and then checked it for any messages.

After that was done, I lay in bed and stared at the ceiling. I still didn't feel guilty for what I had done to Brian. I was standing up for myself. Not only for what he was doing at that moment, but standing up after not having been able to for years. Brian had been a bully to me since elementary school, and now I wasn't going to have to worry about him any longer.

It was like a huge weight had been lifted off my shoulders. It'd been a long time since I'd felt so relieved.

I still felt a bit of worry, however. What if Brian woke up and he knew that I was the new superhuman? What would he do? Would he go to the press? He was going to be mad and want revenge. I hoped he didn't remember any of it at all. But then again, if he didn't remember that I was the one who had beaten him, he'd just go right back to being a bully to me again.

Suddenly the relief left and the weight piled itself back onto me, and I felt as if I'd made a terrible mistake.

CHAPTER 11

CLEARED FOR LIFTOFF

I STOOD IN OUR barn, the early morning light seeping through the open doors. Most of the animals were outside save for a chicken or two, so I had plenty of room to practice using my superpowers.

I stood with my arms to my sides, and my hands stretched outwards. I jumped in the air, but my feet came back to the ground less than a second later. "Okay," I said to myself. "That one didn't work."

I changed my tactic and tensed my legs up. I didn't know what to do after that, though. *Maybe try jumping again?* I thought. So I did, and again, nothing.

"Dammit!" I cursed out loud. I had no idea what I'd done to fly the first time. It was just a gut reaction that I'd had when I saw someone was in danger. The thought crossed my mind that maybe flying was something I could only do when it was a life or death situation, which would suck because I didn't particularly enjoy those situations, but I did enjoy flying.

I decided that maybe it had something to do with the mind. I closed my eyes and slowed my breathing, only taking long, deep breaths. I didn't even try to think about flying until

I was completely relaxed and aware of everything around me. Once I'd achieved that, I began to picture myself being lifted off the ground. I imagined what it would feel like to be no longer touching the ground. My mind went back to a couple of days ago, when I'd flown to save Macy. What it had felt like: the wind blowing through my hair, my clothes flapping in the wind.

That was when I realized it.

My eyes flew open, and I looked down. I was floating four feet off the ground. I smiled from ear to ear, and started laughing to myself. I couldn't believe it. I was actually flying. Well, floating, technically.

I leaned forward, and my heart skipped a beat, my brain not comprehending what was going on. I lay flat in the air. My hands were still at my sides, but I couldn't resist taking my right hand, making a fist, and pointing it in front of me. I willed myself forward, and slowly flew to one end of the wall, where I tapped the wood with my fist. I turned myself around, and flew to the other end. I spent the next few minutes flying back and forth, trying to figure out how it all worked.

Next I started flying at an angle, getting practice moving up and down. The really scary part came when I decided to practice flying straight up and down. Touching the ceiling of the barn was easy, but flying straight down to touch the ground? My brain was freaking out, and my stomach was twisting. There was something about being upside down and flying straight toward the ground that was a little bit freaky. I couldn't quite wrap my head around it.

"You get clearance from the FAA for this flight?" Dad asked me.

I could see his upside down figure standing at the entrance

of the barn. I lifted myself up a bit, flipped upright, and then lowered myself to the ground. My footing was a bit wobbly at first, but it only took a few seconds for me to adjust. "I don't think so," I said with a chuckle.

"Try not to destroy anything," Dad said.

"I'll try," I told him. I walked over to a bottle of water that I'd set next to one of the beams holding up the upper loft of the barn. I took a swig from it, and Dad took a few steps closer to me. He leaned against the beam a few feet away from me.

"What other tricks you got in there?" he asked.

"Well," I began as I threw the bottle of water back to the ground. "So far I've got strength, flight, invulnerability, speed, and super hearing."

Dad scoffed. "That's it? No laser vision? Freeze breath?"

I shook my head. "I think I might be able to take a couple people out with the morning breath I've got, but that's about all I'm going to be doing with that."

"Well, beggars can't be choosers, I guess," Dad said with a smile.

I laughed. "I guess not."

"Your mom went to town to grab a couple of things. You wanna go inside and watch some videos of Richter?" Dad asked.

I looked at him, confused. "What for?"

Dad shrugged. "Well, you know, 'know thine enemy' and stuff. I think it'd be a good idea to see what you're up against."

I gulped and felt my palms begin to sweat. I didn't like the idea of having to go up against Richter. I knew I'd have to, but it seemed like something that was far off. The way Dad was acting made it feel like I was going to have to face him tomorrow. Still, I knew he was right. I needed to figure Richter out the best I could. Because the next time I wouldn't have the element of surprise on my side.

"Yeah, okay," I said. I leaned over and gathered my things.

"Great," Dad said. "Let's hurry before your mom gets back. She's still really freaked out by all of this. Wouldn't want to worry her any more."

I nodded. "Yeah, I gotcha."

Dad and I walked the rest of the way to the house in silence, both of us deep in thought.

When we walked in, I sat down on the couch and put my feet up. Dad already had YouTube pulled up on the television and had his first clip ready to go. He stood by the TV like he was a teacher showing a video to his class, and I was his superhuman student.

"Okay, so this first video is Richter's very first public appearance," Dad began. "It's a couple of months old, but he hasn't evolved his style any. That's good, because it means he's still cocky and full of himself, which means he makes more mistakes. Although I'm sure his ego's a bit bruised after your encounter with him," Dad said, trying to hide the smile of pride he had for me.

"But it's also bad, because now he feels like he has something to prove," I said, bursting his bubble.

Dad raised a finger, waving it in agreement. "This is true, but I feel like you'll still be able to use his attitude to your advantage. Anyway," Dad said, turning to the television. "Let's watch this clip."

He pressed a button on the remote, and the video began to play. It was a cell phone video showing Richter walking out of a bank in Manhattan carrying sacks filled with money. An officer got in the way, so Richter kicked him, sending him flying off screen and surely to his death. The other officers opened fire on him, but the bullets ricocheted off his body.

Richter put down his bags, waited for a moment, seemingly to collect his thoughts, and then in a split second appeared next to one of the police officers at the front of the barricade. He grabbed him by the throat and threw him straight into the air. Then he picked up the police officer's car and crumpled it up a bit in the back to make it easier to hold. When the police officer he'd thrown moments ago started coming back down, Richter flew up a few feet to meet him. He swung the officer's car like a bat, hitting the officer with tremendous force. The man exploded, showering the crowd with blood.

Richter threw the car down into another group of officers then grabbed another officer and threw him through a building. He continued his rampage until all the officers were dead.

He walked calmly back to the sacks of money he'd put down earlier and picked them up. He was about to fly away when he caught a glimpse of the person hiding underneath a table outside a restaurant, the one who'd been recording the whole thing. His glowing blue eyes looked into the camera. In a blur, Richter appeared in front of the man in a split second. The man let out a yell, startled. Richter threw the table aside and the man dropped his camera. It was impossible to see how, since everything went black, but you could hear the man screaming, and then silence as he was presumably killed.

Richter picked the cell phone up off the ground and pointed it at himself. At first you couldn't see anything because his glowing blue eyes were blowing out the camera. Once the exposure adjusted, though, you could see his black hair was matted red with blood, and his face was stained brown and red. "My name is Richter," he said; his voice was that of a young adult and carried no remorse. "That is the only name that matters."

There was a crushing sound and the video stopped, Richter having presumably destroyed the phone.

I felt nauseous and my head spun. While pretty much everybody on the planet had watched that video millions of times, I'd never been able to watch the whole unedited thing. Just the safe-for-TV version they played on the news. Seeing the officers being killed, and the ease with which Richter had done so, terrified me. I had no idea how I was going to be able to go up against him.

I was the only person on Earth who'd ever been able to do damage to Richter. It was up to me to stop him. And I was absolutely terrified. All I wanted to do was to run or fly away and hide.

"So," Dad began. He crossed one hand across his body, and with his other he held up his chin. "Thoughts?"

"Ummm... how about 'what the hell'?" I asked.

"Well, I hope you got more from it than that," Dad said.

I sat back into the couch and looked up at the ceiling. "I was a little distracted by Richter killing all those officers. I wasn't really paying attention."

I could see Dad nod from the corner of my eye. "Well, we're going to watch it again."

I sat up. "Watch it aga—" I began to protest, but Dad stopped me.

"Yes, watch it again. You need to be learning from this. It's up to you to stop the deadliest man on the planet, Kane. You need to study him, learn from him, do whatever you can to stop him. I know it's not a fun video to watch, but it needs to be done." Dad turned and looked out the windows. The ones he'd had to replace, thanks to Richter. "You're my son, Kane. I don't want you going out there at all, but I know you have to. And if you're going to, I want to know that you're as prepared as you can possibly be. That I did what I could."

I had to look away from Dad. I couldn't bear it. I knew this had to be so difficult on him, seeing me go through everything. I knew I had to give it my all, for him. "Okay, Dad," I said.

Dad turned to look at me, his eyes glistening.

I nodded. "Let's watch it again."

CHAPTER 12

THE CALM BEFORE THE STORM

I SET DOWN THE tractor as easily as I could, trying my best not to damage anything.

"Anything else?" I asked.

Dad looked at me with his mouth slightly open, totally dumbfounded. He shook his head. "N-no. That's the heaviest thing I can think of."

I wiped the grease off on my jeans and then walked over next to Dad. We were both behind the barn where Mom couldn't see us, testing the limits of my powers. So far there was nothing I couldn't handle. I had lifted everything in the barn like it weighed nothing. I could fly and run from one end of our hundred-and-fifty-acre field in just a few seconds, too. We didn't dare run or fly past our property, since we were afraid of attracting any unwanted attention. Plus, I knew the property like the back of my hand, so I didn't have to worry about watching where I was going as much. All I had to focus on was speed.

Still, a hundred and fifty acres isn't that much room to get up to speed. I was eager to get out in the open to see what I could really do. Dad and I both agreed that it wasn't a good idea, though. If anybody got any videos of me and posted them on the Web, you could be sure Richter would be watching it on a loop trying to figure out what he was up against, just like we were doing with him.

"You ready to call it a night?" Dad asked.

"Yep. You know anything as far as dinner?" I asked Dad as we began walking back into the house.

"I think your mom grabbed some pizza."

"Yes! Pizza sounds so good right now. Did she get it from the grocery store, or did she get some from Yorkshire Pizza?"

Dad smiled and laughed. "She didn't get any shitty frozen pizza, she got some from Yorkshire!"

I tried to say something in response, but I was speechless. My father had just casually cursed in front of me. That was something he only did if he was angry, or if it was part of a joke he was telling, or some sort of special occasion like that. His dropping an S-bomb casually in a conversation like that was definitely breaking new ground, and it made me very happy. I still didn't have the guts to say it back, but it made me feel good knowing my father was looking at me as more of a grownup. I guess a day of bonding over testing out your son's superpowers does that to a father.

*

"These are some nice digs you got going on here. You should get thrown off a roof by a supervillain more often. Better yet, let him throw *me* off one!" Drew exclaimed as we stepped into Macy and her sister's new apartment.

Macy rolled her eyes as she gave Drew a hug.

"You're an idiot, Drew," Michael said as he walked in

behind him and handed Macy some flowers. "These are from all of us."

Macy took a look at them and smiled. They were what the florist had described as a "summer assortment," made up of sunflowers and some purple and yellow and white other flowers. But sunflowers were the only ones I recognized.

"I love them!" she all but shrieked. "Thank you, guys, so much."

She turned to me and gave me a big hug. I took in a deep breath, inhaling the wonderful smell of her perfume. She broke free of our embrace all too soon and closed the door behind me.

"Thank you all so much," she said again. "I really don't know what I'd do without you three as my friends."

"Aww, shucks, Macy," Drew said. "You're not bad yourself."

"I thank what he's trying to say is thank *you*, Macy. You're a wonderful member of our crew," Michael said.

"And I think what *he's* trying to say is thank *you* for being such a great friend yourself," I said.

All four of us burst out laughing. Macy walked over to the kitchen and pulled a vase out of a cabinet, filled it with water, and put the flowers inside. "There," she said as she placed the vase in the middle of the counter. "They look perfect."

I smiled. They did look perfect. And so did Macy. She was wearing a green T-shirt that made her green eyes explode with color, and black yoga pants that made her look flat-out *hot*. God, I was so in love with her. She really was the most beautiful girl I'd ever seen.

"Where's the big sis?" Drew asked.

"She's out with some friends," Macy said as she walked

out of the kitchen and back toward the entryway where we were all standing. "Come into the living room, guys."

The three of us walked into the living room and sat down on the leather couches that were in an L-formation. A giant TV sat in the corner on top of a glass television stand.

"Nice TV," I said.

Macy smiled. "Oh, thanks. Like most everything in here, it was donated."

"Hey, if you've got any extras, you can send them my way," Drew said.

"Didn't you just get a new TV?" Michael asked, slightly perturbed.

"That's not the point."

Macy laughed and shook her head. "Sorry, but anything extra I donated to the Richter Relief Fund."

The RRF was not just a fund, it was a charity that helped people get their lives back together after their homes and/or families had been destroyed by Richter. At least, that's what they did in theory. Since Richter was currently going full throttle, there hadn't really been a chance for recovery or relief just yet.

Yet another reminder that I was the only one who was going to be able to bring about said relief and recovery.

"What's the plan for tomorrow?" Michael asked.

"We haven't even gotten to the plan for tonight," Drew said.

Michael rolled his eyes. "I know that. It was a little bit rhetorical, but also I like to be really organized, okay? You know that!"

"What did you have in mind, Michael?" Macy asked before Drew could jump back in.

"I was thinking we'd go back down to high school and volunteer there some more. I want to still go down there, you know, even though Macy and Madeline aren't there anymore."

I smiled and nodded. "Of course, Michael."

"Yeah, Michael, of course," Macy agreed.

Drew rolled his eyes. "And Big Mike wins the hearts of millions once again."

I chuckled, and Michael let out a smile.

"Let's get to the dinner and shitty TV movies, shall we?" Drew said as he stood and clapped his hands together.

We each grabbed a hamburger that Macy had gotten from the Burger Shack, along with a soda from the fridge. When we turned the TV on, however, my appetite instantly went away.

The channel was on a news station, and on it was an aerial view of an abandoned Manhattan. Richter had taken some buildings and arranged them to spell *REMEMBER MY FAMILY* in the rubble.

"We're not sure who the message from Richter is for," the news lady said. "But speculation is rampant, and it's obvious that we aren't going to get a statement from Richter himself."

I knew exactly who the message was for, though. It was meant for me.

Richter was trying to tell me to remember what had happened to his parents, but little did he know that it was something I was unable to forget. The public killing his family was something that was always in the back of my mind. The fact that the public would most likely do the same thing to my parents if they knew who they were was one of my greatest fears. And Richter had reminded me of it using the rubble of Manhattan. He was trying to paint the general population as the bad people, and himself as the victim. While it did make me feel sorry for his family, it didn't make me feel sorry for Richter. He'd killed thousands, and deserved none of my or anybody else's sympathy.

The fact that he was trying to communicate with me was terrifying, however. This was all real. It was happening.

And it was all about to kick off sooner than I thought.

CHAPTER 13

SUITING UP

I PRACTICALLY KICKED THE door to my house down as I charged into our living room. "Mom? Dad?" I shouted.

"In here!" I heard them shout from the kitchen.

I passed the living room to my left and entered the large den area. I almost used my super speed to run to the kitchen, but I showed some restraint. I entered the kitchen and gave Mom and Dad a big hug. Once we were done, I turned to the TV mounted underneath the cabinet and clicked to the news channel.

"It's everywhere, honey," Mom said.

"I know," I said. "He's calling me out."

"What are you going to do?" she asked, her voice shaking.

I turned and looked at Dad, who seemed to be as clueless as I was.

I stood there for a moment, thinking. "I'm not going to play his mind games," I said finally. "He can send all the messages he wants. But until I see him out there... just... being Richter, I'm not going out there. I have to train as much as I can before I face him."

Dad nodded. "You're going to let him come to you, not you go to him," he said, summing up what I was trying to say in a way that made sense.

"Yeah, exactly."

"Wait here," Mom said abruptly. She walked out of the kitchen and disappeared around the hallway and into her and Dad's bedroom.

I looked at Dad, confused. Dad just shrugged, acting as if he had no idea what Mom was talking about. I could tell by the smug look on his face, though, that he knew.

Mom came back into the kitchen holding a white cardboard box, the kind you put clothes in before you wrap them up and give them as a gift.

"What's this?" I asked as she handed it to me.

"Just open it!" she said with a smile.

I pushed aside some mail that sat on the kitchen counter and set the box down. I slid my fingers underneath the sides and lifted the top of the box off.

Folded neatly inside was a navy blue suit with scarlet-red stitching. I let out a small gasp as I pulled the suit from the box. I unfolded it and marveled at its beauty.

The chest, shoulders, and part of the back were a thick, rough navy leather and had a scarlet stitching outline. The pants part of the suit was leather as well, but unlike the roughness of the leather on the chest, was surprisingly smooth to the touch. The rest of the suit was made up of an extremely thin and lightweight material that didn't hinder my dexterity or range of motion. There was a headpiece as well, which covered my entire skull except for my eyes, and from my chin up to a hardened nosepiece. Also in the box were a pair of navy blue sneakers—with scarlet-red shoelaces, of course—and a pair of leather gloves.

"Wow," I said as I held the suit up to my body. "This is incredible, Mom!"

Mom smiled and looked me over, looking very proud. "I know how worried you are about keeping your identity a secret. It's not bulletproof, and it doesn't have any special gadgets or anything like that, but it'll get the job done. Nobody will know who you are, and we'll all be safe."

Dad gave me a pat on the shoulder. "Plus, you need something iconic. When people see that suit, they'll know that they're safe."

I smiled and laughed. "I guess you can say it's all part of the Kane Andrews brand."

Dad rolled his eyes and Mom laughed.

"Yes," Dad said. "I guess you could say that."

I stood there for a moment admiring the suit before Mom waved her hands toward the bathroom. "Go try it on! I worked hard sewing that thing together. I want to see how good it looks on you!"

"Alright, alright!" I said as Mom ushered me to the bathroom.

I shut the door behind me and flicked on the lights. I was only wearing a white T-shirt and some basketball shorts, so I didn't bother taking those off. I figured the suit would probably be a bit more comfortable with those on.

I put on the suit like a SCUBA diver would put on his wetsuit. From the back, I stuck my legs into the leather pants, which, while being tight, were surprisingly comfortable and thankfully offered a lot of room around the crotch area.

Next I slipped my head into the mask part of the suit,

then stuck my arms into the sleeves. I reached behind me and, thanks to my increased dexterity, zipped the suit up with ease. I took a moment to admire myself in the bathroom mirror.

Damn, I looked badass.

The fabric that wasn't leather was form fitting, so you could see the outlines of my abs and biceps, which were growing larger with each passing day. The headpiece worked perfectly, as there were no defining features showing. My eyes weren't glowing, however, so I focused on them, and, like flipping a switch, they began to glow bright. Now it'd really be impossible to tell who I was.

I slipped on the navy blue leather gloves and was surprised at how thin they were and how little they restricted my movement.

Once they were on, I took one last look at myself in the mirror. The outfit was complete, and I was beginning to feel ready for whatever Richter would throw my way.

I wasn't. Not in the slightest.

Chapter 14

Richter Returns

I'LL NEVER FORGET the moment when everything I'd been dreading came to life.

I was sitting on the couch, messing around on my phone with the television playing in the background. I wasn't really paying attention to the TV, as I was in the middle of a nice text conversation with Macy.

The Breaking News jingle played, and the news reporter began her spiel. "We have breaking news for you coming out of Ebon, Indiana. We have reports coming in from eyewitnesses all over the city saying that Richter is in the middle of wreaking havoc. Unfortunately we cannot be more specific than that, but local news teams are on their way to safely get coverage. Many of you are familiar with the city of Ebon, after reports of a second superhuman surfaced in recent days, one who actually scared Richter off. There's speculation that this is a move by Richter to try to draw out this second Super, but as this story is still developing, there's no way for us to know for sure. It'll be interesting to see how this will all play out, so you don't want to turn the channel."

"Kane! What are you doing?" my dad shouted at me, breaking me from my trance.

I looked at up him, and he was trying his best to keep his composure and not freak out.

"I'm scared, Dad," I said, barely above a whisper. I thought I was going to throw up. My palms were practically dripping with sweat, and I couldn't find the strength to stand.

Dad walked over to me, got down on one knee, and put his hand on my shoulder. He looked into my eyes and smiled. "I believe in you, son. I've never been more proud of anyone than I am of you right now. Go out there and make me even more proud."

I felt a warmth wash over me. My dad believed in me, and that gave me more strength than superpowers ever could.

I nodded. "Okay. I guess it's my time to shine."

I heard Mom clear her throat, and I looked up at her. She'd walked into the room while Dad and I were having our moment, and was standing in the entryway holding my suit. She opened her mouth to say something, but her voice just cracked. Instead, she held out my suit.

I stood up and walked over to her. I took it from her hands and then gave her a hug.

I let go of her and then pulled the suit on over my clothes. I put it on so fast Mom and Dad couldn't even see me do it. To them, I was their son one second, and someone in a super suit the next.

"Keep an eye on the news," I told them as I walked to the front door.

"Don't worry. We'll be glued to our seats, cheering you on from here," Dad said.

I smiled at them and then walked out the door. I stood on

the front lawn and took a deep breath. *It's showtime,* I thought before launching into the air and beginning my flight to Ebon.

It took only a few seconds to reach Ebon, but that's all it took to shift my focus away from my parents and on to finding Richter.

Ebon isn't a very large city, so it took only two quick scans before I saw Richter hovering a few hundred feet over downtown. He was a couple of miles away, but with my super hearing mixed with his amplifying his voice, it wasn't hard to hear what he was saying at all.

"You're out there, come face me. I will tear this city apart if I have to in order to find you. And if you're not here, I will tear down another, and another, and another. I'll tear this whole damned world apart if I have to."

Well, you're not going to have to, I thought. I focused in on Richter and launched myself right at him, fists at the ready.

I flew as fast as I could, which was a huge mistake. There was a loud sonic boom as I broke the sound barrier, which gave me away to Richter. Given his own super-speed and reflexes, he was able to duck down. As I flew over him, he reached up and grabbed my suit, and, using my momentum against me, he shifted my course and sent me spiraling straight toward the ground.

I threw on the brakes as hard as I could, but I didn't have much room to stop. I stopped myself just inches from a cameraman who had his giant camera pointing directly at my face. I was thankful for my suit and glowing eyes, because if it weren't for them, my face would've been filling the screens of televisions and computers around the world.

I turned around just in time to see Richter barreling down at me, going full speed. Using my speed and reflexes, I kicked him right in the jaw once he got in range. That knocked him off course, so instead of his crashing into me and, subsequently, the camera crew behind me, he went flying through a ten-story building that was in the middle of construction. Part of the building collapsed, sending dirt flying everywhere and dust billowing into the street.

"Shit!" I shouted, angry with myself. I might have saved the camera crew, but sending Richter through a building wasn't exactly the safest thing ever. I hoped that the construction crew had the day off, or were in the side of the building that hadn't collapsed.

Richter used that distraction to his advantage. It felt as if I'd been hit by a freight train as Richter barreled into me as fast as he could, and he wasn't stopping. I was in too much shock and pain to fight back as the world flew by around me at Mach speed. Richter pulled me back and then threw me down into a mountain. A deafening boom shot through the air as the earth exploded around me. The side of the mountain had been obliterated by my impact, and I was lying at the bottom of a giant hole I'd punched into the earth.

I screamed in pain as I felt my bones pop back into place and fuse back together. Bones that had been obliterated and turned to dust regrew in a matter of seconds. I was alive, but just barely. My body repaired itself just enough to keep it that way, but judging by the blood I was coughing up and the incredible amount of pain I was in, it'd be a while before I was fully recovered.

The hole I was in was filled with dust, but the sides were perfectly round and smooth, as if someone had taken a hole-puncher and punched a perfect hole into the ground. I looked up, and I could barely see a pinhole of light far, far away. That tiny pinhole was actually the hole leading to the surface, and I would later find it was a hundred yards wide.

A pair of glowing eyes descended into the hole. Even though it was too dark to see his face, I knew it was Richter. He picked up my limp body, and I didn't have the energy to protest or fight back. I was in too much pain.

Richter carried me out of the hole and dumped me at the edge of it as soon as we got outside. I coughed up some dust and tried to get as much oxygen in me as I could. The oxygen and fresh air must have sped up my recovery, because I was already feeling much better, much faster.

"When you're ready to stand, I'm ready to talk," Richter said as he sat down next to me, dangling his feet over the edge of the pit my body had formed.

I took a few more deep breaths, and, while trying not to scream in pain, I pushed myself up to my feet. I stumbled a bit like I was drunk, but I eventually found my footing. I could feel my insides repairing themselves much quicker now, and my pain was being replaced with anger.

Richter stood up and chuckled. "There we go."

I took a few wobbly steps toward him and yelled "You son of a bitch!" as I swung my fist at him as hard as I could. Even though I wasn't at a hundred percent, it was still a punch fast enough that most people wouldn't see it coming, and hard enough that it would most definitely kill you.

Still, Richter dodged it with ease, weaving and bobbing his head out of the way like a professional boxer.

I tried to swing again, but Richter pushed me, sending me flying a hundred miles an hour into a boulder. My spine cracked and broke again. I tried to yell in pain but was paralyzed for a split second. My spine snapped back into place, repairing itself.

Richter was by my side in the blink of an eye. "Now, I can do this all day. You, on the other hand, look like you're in a lot of pain. Trust me, you'll get used to it. We can save the 'getting used to it' for a later date, though. Right now, I just want to have a discussion, if that's alright with you. Or would you like for me to send you down the side of another mountain? We're in Washington right now, and there's lots of 'em to choose from."

I gritted my teeth, rage filling every inch of my body. I spat on the ground next to Richter. "I don't have anything to say to you."

Richter sighed. "Alright, here we go." He picked me up, about to take me on another painful ride.

"Wait!" I didn't want to have to go through pain like that again. "Okay," I said through heavy breathing. "Let's talk."

CHAPTER 15

THE MOUNTAINTOP

I SAT ACROSS FROM Richter when his eyes stopped glowing. I could see his face clearly and fully. There was a bit of dirt on it, and his longish hair covered part of his eyes until he brushed it aside. He smiled, giving me a toothy, pearly-white grin. His eyes were a deep brown and—for lack of a better phrase—filled with a boyish charm. Like he'd just gotten a new toy for Christmas and was moments away from tearing it open to play.

"So you're the new kid on the block," he said, examining my battered body. "Your suit's a little torn." He poked at my skin through a hole in the side.

I flinched away, but instantly regretted showing any weakness.

"What's with the suit, anyway? You think you're some sort of hero?" Richter let out a laugh. "That's ridiculous. You're no *superhero*." He spat the word out like it was venom.

"I'm better than you," I said through gritted teeth.

"Oh, really?" Richter turned and looked at the damage we'd done to the mountain. It was almost totally blown apart, more of a crater than a mountain. "Because I think there's a mountain around here somewhere that would disagree with you," Richter said. He laughed, proud of his joke.

"What do you want, Richter?" I asked.

Richter raised a hand. "Please, call me Patrick."

"Just tell me what you want to talk about, *Richter*."

Richter's joking expression flashed red with anger, but he was able to hold it back. "I have a proposition for you...." He looked at me questioningly. "What's your name, anyhow?"

Now it was my turn to laugh. "You think I'd tell you?"

Richter shrugged. "Worth a shot, no? Anyway, as I was saying. A proposition." Richter cleared his throat and stood. He paced in front of me. "You and I are both special. We're different. We're *better*. We could basically do anything we wanted to, with no one to stop us. Or at least I can. I have, as I'm sure you've seen. I've turned the world into my playground. But to be honest," Richter said as he turned and looked at me, "it can get kind of lonely."

"And I care about your loneliness why?" I asked, trying to make jabs at him. If I couldn't hurt him physically, I'd at least try to let my words do some damage.

"Because," Richter began as he crouched down to get eye level with me. I was still sitting against a boulder, letting my body heal. "Soon you'll be lonely, too. You'll try to hide your powers, try to keep your loved ones safe." Richter's face turned dark. "But then you'll start to feel a disconnect. Your friends will start to push you away, saying you've been acting 'weird,' that you've been 'hiding something,' that they can't 'trust you.'" Richter was trying to keep himself from shaking with anger. "BUT YOU'LL JUST BE TRYING TO PROTECT THEM!" he yelled, his words filled with anger.

I jumped up from my seat, and Richter stood as well. "So

the next step for you was to go on a rampage?" I said back, as smug as I could.

"No!" Richter snapped. "It was to tell them who I was. But they said I was a *freak*. They were *afraid*. But you know what?" Richter got a crazed look in his eyes. "They were right. They were right to be afraid of me. They were right in calling me a freak. Because I am a freak. I'm a freak who's better than them. Who's better than every person on this goddamned Earth." Richter's voice turned soft; the charm returned to his eyes. "And together, you and I could rule this place. The Earth can be our playground. We could have whatever we want. *Who*ever we want. So let's not fight. Don't make me have to kill you. Because we could have so much fun."

I couldn't believe what I was hearing. Richter thought that what he was doing was actually fun. He'd lost his humanity. He'd lost his reason to live. Well, replaced it would be a better word. Now his reason to live was to have fun by destroying the Earth. His superpowers had driven him mad, and that terrified me.

"So, what do you say?" Richter said, extending his hand. "Truce?"

I looked at his hand. I couldn't believe someone who was only seventeen held the world in such a state of constant fear, and his hand was just inches away from mine. He wanted me to shake it. My gaze turned to Richter's eyes, and I could feel my anger and rage toward him fill mine.

I let my emotions well up inside me. This man had killed so many, destroyed the lives of many others, and had just gotten done asking me to join him—*after* beating the shit out of me. I was so angry at him, I had to have been shaking. I made a fist and did something that felt amazing.

I punched Richter as hard as I could, square in the face. I let out a yell so loud and punched him so hard that a shock wave blew dust and small pebbles back.

Richter went flying backwards into the Washington forest. He took out many trees as he slid for a good mile or two across the ground, screaming in pain the entire way.

The bones in my arm healed themselves almost instantly, and I took to the skies, flying back to Ebon as fast as I could, thankful to have survived another encounter with Richter. I knew, though, that it would most certainly not be my last.

Things were only getting started.

CHAPTER 16

TWO SIDES TO THE TRUTH

I HOVERED TEN THOUSAND feet above my house, scanning as far as the eye could see for any sign we were being watched. I could see everything clearly, even from my height. And by everything I mean nothing, since there was not a soul for miles around. All attention was on Ebon; no one suspected the small farm just outside its borders to be where I lived.

I flew down and landed in the backyard. I practically limped to the back door and walked inside. My entire body ached and I felt very sore. However, it occurred to me through all of the discomfort I was in that I had no idea what to say to announce my arrival. Was I just supposed to yell, *Hey, Mom and Dad! I'm home! Back from fighting Richter. We destroyed a mountain and stuff?*

Before I could decide, though, Mom came running from the living room and into the entryway for the back yard.

"Kane?" she said as she came around the corner.

I realized my eyes were still glowing, and I turned them off just in time for hers to meet mine.

"Oh my God!" she shouted as she ran to me and hugged me. "Andy, get in here!" she yelled to my dad.

My dad came to see what was going on, and his face was practically glowing he was so proud of me. He walked over to me, and Mom let go of me so Dad could give me a quick hug.

"You looked good out there," Dad said.

"Oh, yeah?" I winced in pain at the thought of what I'd just gone through. "It sure felt like I had my ass handed to me."

Mom brought her hand up to her mouth, fighting back tears.

"The important thing is that you got Richter away from the city. You let people know your intentions, and that's what's most important." Dad had a sly smile on his face. "Who knows? People just might start to hope again."

*

Three days after the fight with Richter, it was still all over the news. Everyone was talking about it on social media too. I stood in the kitchen leaning up against the bar with my phone out, scrolling through one of the many Trending Topics on Twitter that had to do with our battle. (Although I wasn't really sure you could call it a "battle" when really he just beat the crap out of me, then we talked for a bit.) Thankfully there were no cameras in the Washington State mountains, because a lot of people would be very disappointed, and they *definitely* wouldn't be calling it a battle.

I had a feeling that they'd be getting the real battle they wanted eventually, though.

"Suit's ready," Mom said as she walked into the kitchen, breaking me from my train of thought.

I looked up. "Oh, yeah? Thanks, Mom."

She pulled a glass from the counter and began filling it with water. "It was a real pain to patch up. Try not to get it so torn up again, alright?"

I chuckled. "I'll try, Mom." I had a feeling she meant that more because a torn-up suit meant I'd been in danger, and not because it meant a lot of work for her.

Mom took a couple of gulps of water before placing the glass down on the counter. "Where's your dad?" she asked as I turned my attention back to my phone and its Twitter feed.

"I think I heard him say he had to do something with the horses." I began to check out of the conversation and pick up my reading pace. I was able to go through a tweet every second. My phone was having a hard time keeping up.

"Will you run out there and ask him what we're doing for dinner?"

"Uh-huh," I said. The tweets were getting good. People were talking about how excited they were about my appearance; how they wished they could be me and give Richter a good punch or two. And I will admit, that last punch I'd given him was pretty solid. I wished there were cameras around to capture *that* Kodak moment.

"Kane!" my mom all but shouted, breaking me from my train of thought.

"Right. Sorry." I locked my phone and put it in my pocket. I lifted up my wrist, clicked the stopwatch feature on my watch, and it began to count.

Everything slowed around me as I began to run toward the door with my super speed. Running so fast was almost like being teleported to another world. Everything around me was in slow motion, and had its own brand-new beauty.

I opened the front door and ran through it, closing it softly behind me. If I were to accidentally slam it, it'd probably bring the house down.

One second.

I ran down the driveway, and onto the worn path in the grass that led to our large red barn.

Two seconds.

I looked out at the horses, who seemed to be frozen mid-stride. They were no doubt galloping, feeling as free and fast as the wind. I smirked at the idea. If only they knew that I was going so fast that to me it seemed like they weren't moving at all. But they were horses, so I began laughing at how exactly I would explain that to them.

Three seconds.

I ran into the barn and came to a stop. I stopped the stopwatch.

"How fast was that?" Dad asked me as he closed the gate on the goat pen. He wasn't even facing me; he could tell it was me by the sudden gust of wind.

"Three seconds," I said, disappointed.

"Why do you sound so disappointed that you ran two hundred yards in three seconds?" Dad said with a laugh.

I shrugged. "I don't know. It'd just be nice to be faster than a bullet or something. I'm sure those things would hurt like hell."

Dad laughed. "Wow, son, I'd be happy to be able to run as fast as I did in high school. I was one of the best running backs my high school had ever seen." Dad had a glimmer in his eye just thinking about it. He wiped his hands on a rag as he walked over to me. The two of us began walking back to the house.

I felt a twinge of guilt nag at me. "Yeah, you're right. Sorry. I just want to be the best I can, you know?"

Dad nodded and put his right arm around me. "I think you're still doing pretty good."

"I know, I just wish pretty good was enough. I need to push myself if I'm going to stop Richter."

"Well, Richter's really the only person you can practice on, so don't take it out on yourself, alright?" Dad said with a pat on my shoulder.

I nodded. "Yeah, okay." I admired and was thankful for Dad's intentions, but they didn't really help that much. On one hand, I had all these people talking about how great I was and how much they wished they were me, while on the other hand I knew the truth, and that was that I was nowhere near good enough to beat Richter. The only times I'd been able to get a punch in were if I had the element of surprise on my side, and I knew that it was going to take way more than one or two punches to take Richter down.

"Oh, yeah," I said, remembering what I'd come out to get Dad for, a few feet away from the front door. "Mom wants to know what's for dinner."

"I'm picking up a pizza for your mom and me." Dad turned to face me with one hand on the doorknob. "You, on the other hand, are going to hang out with Macy and every-body else."

I couldn't believe it, but I actually let out a groan. "I really just want to stay home and watch TV, Dad."

Dad shook his head. "No, Kane. You need to see your friends. Go hang out with them. It'll do you some good. Don't forget you're Kane Andrews, not just…" Bewilderment crossed

Dad's face. "Whatever your Super name is. We really need to come up with something."

I nodded in agreement. "Yeah, we do. I'm getting tired of being called 'the other Super guy.'"

Dad opened the door and the two of us walked in. "Oh, really? I kinda like the sound of that. 'The Other Super Guy.' I dig it."

I rolled my eyes. "Please, Dad. You're not funny," I said with a slight smile, letting him know I was being sarcastic.

I went upstairs to my room to get changed out of my basketball shorts and T-shirt. I threw on a pair of jeans and a dark blue Henley, then grabbed my phone to text the gang to let them know I wanted to hang out. Before I could do that, an alert popped up on my phone from one of my news apps.

Breaking News: 15 People Taken Hostage—Mostly Women and Children—Inside Church on Texas-Mexico Border.

My heart skipped a beat.

I ran downstairs. "Mom! Dad!" I shouted.

"Kitchen!" Mom called.

I ran into the kitchen with super speed, causing the two of them to jump when I suddenly appeared in front of them. "I need my suit," I said.

"What for?" Mom asked.

I read them the headline and Mom shook her head the entire time.

"The police can handle it," she said.

"They *might* be able to handle it. This is the Texas-Mexico border we're talking here. The cartel kills people down there all the time. Fifteen people are nothing to them. I know I can save them. It'd not only give me a chance to practice my skills—which I'll remind you are *not* good enough to take on

85

Richter—and it'll let people know once and for all that I'm on their side."

Dad looked at the floor, deep in thought. I could tell by the look on his face that he agreed with me; he was just trying to figure out a way to tell that to Mom.

"I'm going," I said. "Whether you like it—or hell, even whether *I* like it or not—I have to. It's my responsibility." With that, I turned and grabbed my suit off the counter. I put it on as I went out the door and launched into the air, beginning my ten-minute flight to Texas.

Chapter 17

Interference

I HOVERED ABOVE THE warehouse where, just below, I could see dozens of police and SWAT vehicles in the parking lot of the building, along with news vans and their crews scrambling to set up shop. Their flashing lights were pulsating bright as the sun began to go down.

I trained my super-hearing on the command center, listening in to their conversation.

"Two men by the door, and one more that we know of who's the one communicating with us. There's no way to tell how many more there are in the room with the hostages."

"And which room would that be?" an older gentleman with a Hispanic accent asked.

The young man who had been speaking earlier answered. "We believe they're holed up in a manager's office toward the middle of the warehouse. We're in the process of getting cameras on the inside in order to know for sure."

I turned my attention to the warehouse itself. It was a large one, about the size of a football field. There were holes spread out across the ceiling in varying sizes, put there by rust and erosion. Broken windows lined almost the entire upper part of the wall where it met with the ceiling. I flew to the back of the warehouse. I made my eyes stop glowing, not wanting to be seen. I then flew to the ground as fast and quietly as I could, trying my best to stay out of sight.

I leaned against the warehouse, trying to make myself as small as I could. I listened carefully, but didn't hear anybody coming my way. I still had the element of surprise on my side, which had been the thing to thank for any of the small victories I'd had so far. I intended to keep it on my side for as long as possible, although I knew that I'd have to get my hands dirty at some point. I had to if I planned on not having Richter handing my ass to me next time we met.

I tried listening into the warehouse, but all I could hear was people whimpering, trying to hold back tears. There were a couple of whispers, but they were in Spanish. Then I hit the jackpot. One of the hostage takers began speaking into a phone in English.

"What the hell is going on, Beta?" he yelled into the phone. He spoke perfect English, with just a slight Hispanic accent that was only there because he was angry.

"What do you mean, Charlie?" I could hear the man I assumed was Beta say through the phone.

"You're supposed to pay the police to stay off us! I've got over a dozen police and SWAT cars busting down my doors, and it's all on the news."

Beta laughed. "You really think you're all over the news? Who do you think you are, Richter?"

"Stop your laughing! This is no time for jokes! This is serious. You call the police off. You pay them."

"Don't think that I don't know what I am doing," Beta said, his voice growing dark. "You are a measly little gang. The police are busting down your doors because my people didn't pay them. You've served your purpose."

"How can I get my hostage money when the police are about to kill me?" Charlie screamed into the phone.

"Maybe you should've thought of that before you got too comfortable. Neither I nor my people care what you do or what happens to you. You have served your usefulness. I suggest you find a way to get the money to pay the police fast. I have a feeling they aren't going to want to negotiate with you for very much longer." With that, there was a click, and the phone call ended.

Charlie let out a string of words in Spanish, which I guessed were not very nice.

I stopped listening and began to process what I'd just heard. Beta and Charlie were obviously code names, taken from the phonetic alphabet. Beta definitely seemed to be in control of the situation. My guess was that Charlie and his gang used to work for Beta and his people, but Beta had left Charlie high and dry.

I didn't really care to know much more about the situation. All I knew was that there were hostages who needed saving, and I really couldn't have cared less about Charlie and his gang problems.

I stood up tall and began floating up toward the broken window at the top of the warehouse; it was about two stories up in the air. I eased my head up from the bottom slowly, trying to stay hidden.

The warehouse was large and wide open. There wasn't any equipment, since it was abandoned. It was wide-open save for rows of rusty support beams going up to the ceiling spread out across the entire warehouse, and clusters of offices. There were enclosed offices by the front door, some toward the back, and a break room/office combo toward the middle. I could see through the windows of the break room that the lights were on, and lots of people were piled in there. Most of them were on their knees with their hands tied behind their backs, while the rest stood over them with machine guns in their hands, ready to fire. Outside the office, four more gang members stood guard. I looked across the warehouse, and saw two more gang members standing by the front door, looking out through cracks in the wall at the sea of police and SWAT officers, giving updates into the radios on their shoulders. The news crews were now set up, ready to record any action that might happen from a safe distance away.

I sank down and floated just underneath the broken window, out of sight. I needed to think of a game plan. And judging by the way Charlie had been acting while he was on the phone with Beta, I needed to think fast.

Basically my two options came down to whether I wanted to take all the guards' guns, then fight them, or carry the hostages out, then fight off the gang members. Whichever option I choose, I knew that it had to involve me fighting the gang members. Not only did I need to fight them to practice my fighting and tactical abilities, but I really, really, *really* wanted to have a victory. I wanted to be a hero, because so far, I'd just been a super-punching-bag, and I wanted people to know that I meant business.

I decided that the safest thing to do would be a combination of the two main plans I'd come up with so far. I hovered up and flew through the window then floated down as quietly as I could. Once my feet touched the ground, though, I took off running.

It was time for me to show the world what I could do.

CHAPTER 18

PERFORMANCE ANXIETY

I TORE THROUGH THE door to the room, and went straight for the guns. I yanked them out of the gang members' hands as they stood there frozen. It would be a few seconds before they realized that their guns had disappeared, but by the time they did that, I'd already be almost done moving the hostages to safety.

I threw each gun toward the door as soon as it was in my hands. Once they left my hand, they barely moved through the air. Not frozen, but moving slowly, like they were moving through a sea of syrup. They'd fly out the door at full speed once I was no longer moving so quickly, though, so I wasn't worried.

Once the guns were out of the way, I grabbed the first hostage, a young girl about seven years old. I ran across the warehouse, threw open the front door, and set her down by a group of police officers. Her face was frozen with fear, and tears flowed from her eyes in slow motion.

But they began to speed up.

Oh, shit.

I ran back in as fast as I could, but I was beginning to lose my concentration. I wasn't running as fast anymore, so time began to speed up around me. It still moved very slowly, but at about half normal speed, instead of a tenth of it.

I grabbed another hostage and brought her back to safety. I did my best to focus on moving as fast as I could, but I couldn't help but think I was digging myself into a huge hole. I began to wonder if I should've even involved myself at all.

I began to grab the hostages two by two; the gang members began to realize they were disappearing, as their faces turned from being stone-cold to dazed and confused. One of them reached for something inside his coat, and I realized that some of them had to have pistols hidden on their persons. I didn't have time to get the guns away from them, however. I had to focus on getting the hostages out of there. I wasn't going to be fast enough to do it all.

I took a few more out, and came back for the last hostage. A low rumbling sound reached my ears, followed by a loud, deep pop. I looked at the source of the sound and watched as an explosion slowly erupted from the barrel of a gun, aimed directly at the final hostage, a young Hispanic woman in her early twenties. My concentration faltered, and time began to speed up even more. I was moving slower, and the bullet began to pick up speed. It flew spinning out of the barrel of the gun, moving toward the hostage.

I ran toward the bullet, but I was all the way on the other side of the room from it. In a last ditch effort, I dove. It was only fifteen feet from the woman's head, and moving fast. I let out a yell as I came closer and closer, the bullet only inches away from entering the woman. I reached out my hand as the bullet reached the woman's neck. It began to dig itself into her skin, but I was able to pull it out as I flew over, before it could do any real damage. I threw the bullet to my left, and everything returned to full speed as I crashed into the gang member who'd fired the gun, both of us flying into the wall and falling into a heap on the ground.

I looked up and saw all the gang members looking at me, bewildered. To them, only about ten seconds had passed since I had begun disarming them. My head pounded, and I felt confused as what to do next.

The screams of the final hostage shook me out of my haze. She lay curled up on the ground, her hands wrapped around her neck. Her screams were cries of pain, confusion, and fear, all mixed into one.

I jumped up from the ground, flew to her, wrapped my arms around her, and got her out of there. I flew outside and set her down with the rest of the former hostages. The police officers looked at the group of people who had just appeared, their faces as confused as those of the now-freed hostages.

I turned to one of the officers and lowered my voice. "This one is injured," I said. My voice sounded stupid and ridiculous. I was definitely going to have to think of a better solution.

The officers didn't respond; instead they all raised their guns at me and began yelling at me. "Get on the ground!" they screamed.

I rolled my eyes. "I'm on your side," I said. I was trying to say as little as possible, since whatever came out sounded incredibly dumb. I didn't want to use my real voice, though; I didn't want anybody to be able to figure out my identity.

I flew into the air and headed back for the warehouse, hoping the officers had gotten the message to leave me alone. I headed toward the office that the gang was now scrambling inside, trying to get their guns ready, while at the same time trying to figure out what was going on.

My feet hit the ground, and I skidded to a halt in the middle of the room.

The men looked at me, their faces filled with confusion. I began to look each one of them in the eye, slowing turning as I did so. I tried to look tough and instill fear into them. I guess it worked, because some of them ran out of the room, yelling things in Spanish.

In the end, only four remained, including Charlie.

"So this is it?" I asked.

"It's either you or deportation to the worst Mexican prison," Charlie said. "I choose you."

I smirked. "Why not both?"

With that, I ran to him in a split second, my speed having returned. I punched him in the face hard, but not super-strength hard. I was holding back, only hitting him with the power of a normal human.

Charlie stumbled, but quickly regained his composure. He swung at me, but I didn't dodge in time. The punch connected, and I felt an explosion of pain for a split second before my powers began to heal me, taking away all the pain. I punched him back harder this time, angry that he'd gotten one in on me, but also angry at myself for freezing and not dodging in time.

Charlie landed in a heap on the ground, my punch having knocked him out. I reminded myself to tone it down a bit. I could easily take all these guys out in a matter of seconds, but not only was the point of all this to practice my fighting on real targets, I would most likely kill them if I had my powers turned up to eleven.

I turned around, ready to take on the other three, and also making a mental note to make sure I didn't actually hurt Charlie too badly later.

I was met with a fist slamming into the center of my face, sending me faltering back a few steps.

"Move!" one of the men shouted at the guy who had gotten the surprise attack in on me.

He did, and I found myself staring down the barrel of a pistol. The man on the other side of the room fired, and the bullet came flying toward me. I threw my hand up and caught it just inches from my face. I redirected it toward the leg of the man who'd punched me, and quit moving fast, causing time to return to its normal speed.

The man screamed in pain as the bullet tore through his leg. He fell to the ground, out of commission for the rest of the fight.

The other guy with a gun emptied his weapon, but I simply stepped to the right. All the bullets harmlessly flew past me, and the man stared at me, frozen in shock and fear.

The other one in the room wasn't frozen, however. He began to run to the door, having figured out that he wasn't going to be able to defeat me, and that I was just toying with them.

I ran to the door as fast as I could, blocking the man from exiting. He let out a yelp of fear. I could tell he was wracking his brain, trying to figure out how I had suddenly appeared in front of him.

He turned and began running toward one of the windows, but I blocked his path again. This time I'd scared him so much he fell to the ground. He scrambled away from me on his hands and knees, backwards, not breaking eye contact with me.

I began to feel a bit guilty for scaring them so badly, but then I remembered what these men had done. Not only that day, but all the days before it. The countless number of people they had probably killed.

I heard a scream and looked up in time to see the man who had been shooting at me earlier come at me swinging the butt of his pistol straight at my face. Again, I'd gotten distracted, and again, I took an unexpected blow directly to my nose. This time I felt the bones shatter, and fell to the ground. They began to heal themselves almost as soon as they were broken, but still, I could feel the pain for a few agonizing seconds. Before I could get up, the man began kicking me in my sides.

He got in two good kicks before I grabbed his foot and slammed him to the ground. His head hit the ground with a sickening thud. The man began shaking violently, his whole body seizing. Foam shot from his mouth.

My entire body tensed, and I thought I was going to throw up. I began to panic, not knowing what to do. I was still lying on the ground, eye to eye with a man who was having a seizure because of me. I was paralyzed with fear.

"Please," I heard someone say. I looked up and saw the man I had nearly frightened to death looking at me. He was on his knees next to his seizing friend. "Please, I am sorry." His eyes were big, and tears began to fall from them. I realized how young he looked. He couldn't have been much older than me. "Do not let my friend die. We will surrender. Please. Do something."

I realized that I couldn't just leave the man there, and that I had to do something. Even though they were evil people, I was the one who had caused him to be in this situation. I had to try to help sort it out.

I picked the man up in my arms and ran outside as fast as I could. I placed him on the ground next to some paramedics who were checking out some of the hostages.

Everybody jumped back and let out a gasp. "Help him!" I shouted.

The paramedics rushed to the man's side, and I bolted toward the command center that had been set up in the back of a van. Everybody jumped and gasped, just like the paramedics had moments earlier. I rolled my eyes, but it was a reaction that I was going to have to get used to.

"I'm finished," I said. "They're all yours."

With that, I launched myself high into the air, flying away as fast as I could, trying to figure out whether or not I'd made a huge mistake.

CHAPTER 19

ENEMY OF THE STATE

I WALKED THROUGH THE back door of my house and headed straight for the living room. Mom gasped as I walked in. She and Dad were watching my escapade on the news as I collapsed in a heap on the cool leather couch. I was so tired and drained, I felt as if I could sleep for days.

Mom rushed to my side and began checking me for any wounds.

"I'm fine, Mom," I said as I pushed myself up to a sitting position. "Just really worn out."

"You did good, Kane," Dad said, standing with his arms crossed, wearing a big smile.

"Really?" I said, rubbing my eyes. "Because it felt like I did pretty crappy."

Dad shrugged. "Well, I said you did good, not that you did *well.*"

I let out a moan and lay back down on the couch. "I don't feel as if I'm any better now than I was when I left." I wasn't talking to anyone in particular, just thinking out loud.

"What were you expecting, to come back and be better than Richter?" Dad asked as he walked to the recliner next to the couch and sat down in it. He leaned forward in his chair. "You gotta take something from this. Surely there's something you can learn."

"That I need more practice," I said.

"Well, then, that's what we're going to have to do."

I turned my attention to the TV, which was showing the news. They were showing footage of a blue blur running in and out of the warehouse, carrying hostages to safety. I couldn't help but smile.

"Three of the hostage takers are in critical condition after the new Super stormed past police and the SWAT team and took matters into his own hands. The White House released a statement just moments after the situation in Texas ended."

The scene shifted to an image of the president standing behind a podium, most likely deep within a bunker at an undisclosed location, safe from Richter. His tan skin looked weathered and his hair was turning gray. Most of his aging had probably happened in the time since Richter had first appeared.

"The situation in Texas is a tricky one. While we're all happy that there were no casualties and the hostages are safe, it could have gone very differently. I have full confidence that our law enforcement agencies would have done their jobs, and gotten everyone to safety, without the interference of the superhuman we're code naming Tempest, in lieu of an official statement from the superhuman himself."

"Oooh, Tempest. I like it," I said.

My dad nodded. "It sounds badass."

Mom shot him a look for using language, but he ignored it.

The president continued. "We would like Tempest to stop interfering with any government agencies, and allow our trained, professional, and efficient law enforcement personnel to do the work they do best.

"And also, to Tempest, a warning. Should you use your powers in any way, you are effectively making yourself an enemy of the United States of America. We will not have another Richter on our hands. We are working on a solution to the Richter problem, one we hope to resolve shortly. We understand that you're trying to help and do good. But you don't have to be a superhuman to be a hero. So, please, stay out of the way. I will authorize the same measures that will be exercised on Richter to be exercised on you, should the situation call for it.

"Thank you, and may God bless the United States of America."

The screen returned to the news anchor, and she began to comment on the president's statement. I tuned it out, though, as I was processing what I'd just heard.

I was the only person on Earth who'd ever actually hurt Richter, and now they were telling me to back off. It wasn't like anything they'd done helped the situation any! All they'd managed to do was shoot missiles at him that amounted to little more than expensive fireworks. They'd gotten many soldiers killed at the beginning of the chaos, before they knew what they were dealing with. Not that they knew now, apparently, since I was the only one who'd actually gotten anything done.

But now they were telling me that they would hunt me down if I used my powers again. I understood that; they were scared. Richter hadn't exactly set a great example for superhumans. But I was trying to help. Trying to stop him, and save everybody. Trying to do exactly what the government couldn't, yet they were painting me as an enemy. Like I was Richter 2.0 or something.

"We'll figure something out," Mom said, shaking me from my thoughts.

I looked into her eyes, and for some reason, everything seemed to melt away. Mom looked at me with her big eyes, filled with pride. I guess even though she was terrified for me, she still understood why I had to do what I had to do. And she was proud of me for it, and hated to see that I was being punished for doing the right thing.

"Yeah," I said, and nodded. "We will."

I looked up to my dad, who was looking at me with the same look Mom had. He returned my nod. "We will." A sly smile slid across his face, and his expression turned giddy, like a little kid's. "We will, Tempest."

I smiled back at him. Despite everything, I had to say that the government had done a pretty good job picking a kick-ass superhuman name for me.

And it wouldn't be long before they'd see Tempest again.

CHAPTER 20

CONFIDENT CONFESSIONS

DAD WAS INSISTENT that I not get so caught up in being Tempest that I stopped being Kane Andrews, so when Drew invited me to go to a party, I accepted.

Driving to Macy's apartment, where we were all going to meet up before driving to the party, I was overwhelmed with a feeling of nostalgia. I sat in my car listening to the radio, watching the world drive by. It felt normal, which was something I hadn't felt since before Richter had begun his rampage.

I'd felt frightened and afraid then, not knowing if Richter would somehow end the world at any moment. That feeling had been replaced by a feeling of duty and pride whenever my powers manifested... which was replaced by a feeling of pain and eventually betrayal by the people I was trying to help.

But now, driving to meet up with my friends before a party, I felt like a normal teenager. A normal *human being*. I'd forgotten how nice it felt, and I was glad that Dad had insisted I go. I definitely wanted and needed a small break. It wasn't like I had much of a choice, though. The government had their eye out for me, so lying low for a little bit was my best option. I couldn't stop Richter *and* the U.S. Government;

at least that was the excuse I told myself to keep myself from feeling guilty.

After another twenty minutes of driving and singing along with the radio, I reached Macy's apartment. She buzzed me in, and I rode the elevator to the seventh floor. I forgot about everything when she opened the door and I was once again face-to-face with the woman I was very much in love with.

"Hi," she said in a small voice. "Come in." She stepped aside, and I stepped in.

"How are you?" I asked.

"I'm doing well," she said as she walked out of the foyer. I followed close behind.

"Hey, Kane," Madeline said from the kitchen, where she was pouring a protein shake into a bottle.

"Hey," I said. I pointed at the shake. "Going for a run?"

Madeline chuckled. "Stop acting like you're interested in what I'm doing. I know why you're here," she said with a sly smile and nodded toward Macy.

Macy's face turned almost as red as her hair. She shot Madeline a death glare. "Don't you have a workout to go to?"

Madeline grabbed her shake and walked around the kitchen counter. "Alright, alright!" She gave me a pat on the arm as she walked by. "Good to see you, Kane." She shot a knowing smile to Macy, and walked out the door.

"Sorry about my sister," Macy said from her seat on the couch. She fumbled with her hands, nervous.

"Don't be," I told Macy as I walked behind the couch. I leaned on its back. "She's right," I said before I could stop myself. I had no idea what I was doing and tried stopping myself before the next words came out. It was like I was on autopilot, though. "The main reason I'm here is to see you, because I think you're amazing."

Shit.

What did I just do?

"Really?"

I opened my mouth but no words came out. I had to force myself to say something. I couldn't go back now. It was all or nothing. "Really. And I'm, like, ninety-nine percent sure you feel the same way."

Macy looked up at me, her eyes sparkling as she blushed. "Well, I mean, you're not wrong." She looked back down at her hands.

I smiled bigger than I ever had before, and that was saying something, all things considered. I felt as if I was floating on air, and my whole body felt warm.

Then I looked down and realized that I actually *was* floating an inch off the floor. I quickly stopped and fell quietly back to the floor.

"So, you do like me?" I asked.

Macy nodded. "Yeah, I do."

It took a lot of self-control to not take off flying across the globe. I had no idea why I hadn't said something sooner. It was so easy. I'd been afraid to, I guess. But now, I had a confidence that I hadn't had before. Was that considered a superpower? Could I be like, *Yes, I have super-strength, speed, hearing, and super-confidence?*

"Why didn't you say anything earlier?" I said as I walked around the couch and sat down next to her.

She looked at me with her mouth open, trying to find the words. "I was afraid, I guess?" Her gaze wandered to the ceiling.

"I was afraid, too. But what were you scared of?"

Macy took a moment before responding. When she did, it came out in a flood. "I guess I don't know where everything is headed. I mean, I still don't. We don't know when all this Richter stuff is going to stop, and what kind of place the world will be after that. I don't know if Madeline is going to want us to go back to Indianapolis after this. If she does, I have to go with her. I don't want to leave you or Drew or Michael behind, but I didn't want to have anything tying me down, and make it harder to eventually leave."

I tried processing what she was telling me. Talk about getting knocked down a couple of notches. I thought I came to the same conclusion she was alluding to, but I wanted to hear it from her. "So, what are you saying?"

Macy thought for a moment and then leaned over and kissed me on the cheek. "That none of that matters anymore."

My stomach churned with excitement, and heat rushed through my head. I felt a feeling of joy that rivaled what I'd felt when I discovered my powers.

My thoughts were interrupted by a loud buzzing. I turned and looked at the door.

"That must be Drew and Michael. They were riding over here together," Macy said.

I nodded and stood up from the couch. "Okay, then, we should probably go now."

Macy giggled. "Yes, Kane, we probably should."

The two of us exited her apartment and headed for the party.

CHAPTER 21

PARTY CRASHERS

THE CITY LIGHTS filtered through the windshield as we drove to Eric and Veronica Russell's house, where the party was being held. Their parents were out of town, which was rare in those days since most people never left due to the whole Richter situation. That meant fewer summertime house parties, so when word got out about Eric and Veronica's party, it traveled fast.

"Doesn't Drew have a crush on Veronica?" I asked as I turned the car into the neighborhood the party was being held in. The question was rhetorical, of course. Everybody knew about Drew's crush on Veronica.

I looked in the rearview mirror and could see Drew glaring at me. "Come on, Kane. Not cool."

I laughed and shrugged. "You should go for it tonight, bro."

"Yeah, man. Go for it," Michael said, agreeing with me.

"See?" I said. "Michael agrees. Do you agree, Macy?" I glanced over at her in the front seat.

"Yeah, of course. You only live once, or some shit."

"Um, we're a *carpe diem* family, thank you," Drew said, correcting her.

We all laughed as we parked on the side of the road. We climbed out of the car, and I took in the scene.

The house was a large two-story one with Roman pillars holding up the roof covering the large front porch. The neighbors' houses were a good distance away with a thin veil of trees in between, so hopefully we weren't going to have to worry about causing them any trouble. People were talking and laughing on the front porch, holding red cups and beer bottles in their hands. I could hear music coming from inside, but it wasn't turned up loud. From the looks of it, the party was surprisingly tame.

We began walking to the front porch, and I exchanged "hello"s and "how you been?"s with a few people I recognized from school before walking inside and making my way to the kitchen. I pulled a bottle of beer from an ice chest sitting on the counter and twisted the top off. I held it out toward Macy, and she took it.

"Thanks," she said as she took a swig from the bottle and examined the room.

I grabbed my own and began to drink it, the familiar bitter and earthy taste washing over my taste buds and going down smoothly. I looked around the kitchen as well, and took in how nice it was. The counter tops were made of marble, and all the appliances were stainless steel. Finger foods were spread out on the counters, and people were wandering in, grabbing a handful, and then walking out into the living room where the music was playing, or outside to hang out and talk.

"Hey, Kane," I heard a familiar voice say from behind me.

I fought the urge to audibly moan as I turned around and

saw Brian Turner standing a few feet away, towering over me. "Hi, Brian," I said, my voice cold.

"Can we talk?" he asked, motioning his head toward the back door.

I thought about it for a moment, then decided that I might want to listen to what Brian had to say. If he remembered anything about our encounter when I had thrown him into a wall, this conversation could go very badly. I didn't know what I was going to do if Brian remembered and knew who I was.

"Yeah," I said. "We can talk."

"Kane," Michael said, his big hands grabbing my arm. "You need us to come with you?" His eyes moved toward Brian. Michael didn't have to say a word; the look he was sending him made his feelings clear. If Brian did anything, Michael would make him wish he'd been thrown into a wall by a superhuman again.

"Not this time," I said. "I've got it under control." Under normal circumstances, I would've loved to have some backup there with me. However, if Brian did remember, I couldn't have Michael and Drew finding out as well. This conversation needed to be held in private.

I followed Brian out the back door, to a spot in the backyard by some trees. We were about thirty feet from the back of the house, and my heart was beating fast. I could see people on the side and back porches chilling out, but none of them were paying attention to Brian and me. I silently prayed that they weren't able to hear us, because if Brian was about to say what I thought he was about to say, I was going to have to do some damage control, and fast.

"I wanted to say thank you," Brian blurted out.

Well. That was definitely unexpected. "I-I... ummm...." I had no idea what to say. The words escaped me.

Brian raised up his hands, gesturing for me to stop talking. "If you hadn't been walking by at that time and seen me lying there...." Brian's eyes glazed over. "I don't know where I'd be. I could be really brain damaged, or worse."

I think you're definitely brain damaged, I thought to myself. *Either that or I am, and I'm having a hallucination right now.*

Brian put his hand on my shoulder, and it felt real. Definitely not a hallucination. "Thank you, Kane. I wouldn't be who I am today without you."

I opened my mouth, but I still couldn't say anything. Finally I found the words. "You're welcome. Any time."

Brian smiled and nodded. "Yeah, okay, well, that's it." And with that, he walked away.

I stood there totally dumbfounded. Brian Turner had just thanked me for saving his life, even though I was the one who had almost killed him in the first place! I guessed that answered the question about whether or not he remembered what had happened. I still felt bad for pummeling him into a wall, even though I'd just been defending myself. However, I *did* feel slightly less bad, since it all seemed to have turned out alright in the end. Brian Turner was off my back, and it seemed like he was going to be a better person. Yeah, maybe I'd knocked a few of his memories loose, but at least no one had to worry about Brian Turner knocking a few of their teeth loose ever again.

I walked back to Eric's house, sipping my beer and chuckling to myself at the craziness of what had happened. When I walked inside, I saw Drew standing in the kitchen eating some finger sandwiches with Veronica, who was giggling profusely at some joke he'd just told. I smiled to myself, feeling happy for Drew. Sorry for Veronica since she had no idea what she was getting herself into, but still, happy for Drew.

I felt someone tap my shoulder, and turned to see it was Macy. My heart fluttered with joy, and I let out a big grin. "How's the party?"

"Forget that," she said, punching me in the arm playfully. "What the hell did Brian want with you?"

I laughed. "You'll never believe me."

"Try me," she said, scrunching up her nose, causing a cute crease to appear between her eyebrows.

"Okay, but let's go somewhere else," I said.

She wrapped her cold, small hands around mine and began pulling me toward the stairs. "Let's go up here," she said.

I followed her up the stairs and down a hallway lined with rooms. She brought me to one at the end and led me inside. It was a bedroom with a full-size bed and a nightstand with family pictures on it. She led me across the room to a sliding glass door and onto a balcony.

"How'd you know this was up here?" I asked, giving her a playfully suspicious look.

"Oh, you know, Eric and I are dating and this is where he takes all his women to seduce them," she said nonchalantly, which clued me in on the fact that she was joking.

"Ha ha," I said as I leaned on the balcony railing. A hot summer breeze brushed across my face. I took another sip of beer to try to keep the heat at bay.

"So," Macy said as she leaned on the railing next to me. "You gotta tell me what Brian wanted."

I explained what had happened, along with how I couldn't

believe it was happening, and thought that one of us was possibly brain dead.

Once I'd finished telling her, Macy looked at me with the same look of disbelief I imagined I'd had when it was all happening. "Wow," she said. "I guess whoever beat him up literally knocked some sense into him!"

"Yeah, I agree. I wish they'd done it sooner!"

"No kidding! I could barely stand him after knowing him for only a few weeks. I can only imagine what it must've been like dealing with him for years."

I shrugged. "It wasn't that bad. More of an annoyance than anything. Still, every once in a while, he'd remind you who's boss."

But I'm the boss now, I thought. I guess you could say that Brian Turner was really the first villain I'd defeated. But for some reason, I didn't think that Richter would be thanking me over a beer any time soon.

"So, Kane," Macy said as she slid closer to me, to the point where our shoulders were touching.

"So, Macy," I said as I looked down into her eyes with a smile.

"What are you thinking about?"

Without even thinking, I blurted, "How much I want to kiss you right now."

Macy bit her lip and held back a smile. She stood on the tips of her toes, and we both closed our eyes.

Our lips touched, and it felt as if electricity was sparking through me. I didn't get the chance to fully enjoy it, though, as the quick burst of a police siren and the flashing of red and blue lights caused me to open my eyes and then wince at how bright they seemed.

"Oh, shit," Macy breathed.

I grabbed her beer bottle from her hand and threw both bottles far away. I got a little carried away, as they went soaring a good thirty yards.

"Wow," Macy said as she grabbed my bicep. "You have a good arm."

"I think we have other things to worry about," I said as I turned and began walking back through the bedroom.

Macy followed close behind as we went down the hallway and down the stairs. I was going to run for the back door once I got downstairs, but some police officers had already made it inside and had everybody rounded up.

"Alright, everybody!" an officer with black scruff and spiky hair shouted. "This party is over. I want everyone to go home. I have some officers standing outside the door with breathalyzers. If you're too drunk to drive, you will call your parents, tell them where you are and what you're doing, and have them come pick you up. No exceptions." The officer found Eric and Victoria in the crowd. He pointed at both of them. "You two aren't going anywhere. You're both in big trouble."

I cursed under my breath and began filing out the door. I breathed into the breathalyzer, which showed that my blood alcohol level was zero. I'd only had a little bit of beer, but I was expecting at least a .01 or .02. But nothing? I had a feeling my health regeneration power had something to do with it.

Macy and I stood outside for a minute until we spotted Drew and Michael. "I'm driving them home," I told the officer. He let them pass without testing them. Drew stumbled behind Macy and me, but I think he was drunk on love more than anything else. Michael brought up the rear, shuffling slowly, sighing heavily.

We all got in the car and breathed sighs of relief. Michael groaned and Drew let out a whoop.

"This whole night could have gone very badly," I said, more thinking out loud than anything.

Macy nodded. "For sure." She turned and looked at me, her face glowing. "But in a way, it was kinda perfect."

I smirked at her. "Yeah, it was kinda perfect."

CHAPTER 22

DRIVES

I FELT A SENSE of sadness wash over me as Macy left the car and disappeared inside her apartment building.

"So, what was going on between you two?" Drew said from the back seat, his voice slightly louder than usual.

I felt my cheeks blush. "What are you talking about?"

Drew laughed. "Oh, you know what I mean. There was something different. I don't know."

"What I want to know is, what was going on between you and Veronica?" I said, changing the subject.

Drew giggled. "We were talking, is all."

"Oh, yeah?" I said as I pulled onto the road and began driving to Drew's house. "Talking? It looked like it was a little more than just talk. Isn't that right, huh, Michael?"

Michael grunted in response. I looked in the rearview mirror, and could see him holding his pudgy face up with one hand as he stared out the window.

"Anyway," Drew said. "I think something's going on between Macy and you."

"And I think you're drunk," I said. Even though he was right, I didn't want to say anything about what was going on between Macy and me. Mostly because I didn't really understand what was going on all that well, either. I wasn't sure if we were "dating," "talking," "seeing each other," or something in between. Besides, even if I did know, I didn't want to blurt it out without making sure it was okay with her first.

Ah, who was I kidding? If we were officially dating, I'd be shouting it from the rooftops before she even got the chance to tell a soul.

Drew and I talked a bit more on the drive to his house. When we pulled up, Drew almost fell out of the car. I had no idea how he'd gotten drunk so fast at the party. I guess he was an extreme lightweight.

"Alright, I'll see you tomorrow," Drew said before he shut the door.

"Wait, what?" I asked.

"Yeah, I need you to give me a ride to my car."

I nodded. "Oh, okay. See you then."

Drew shut the car door and began sneaking toward his house. I backed out and left before he got inside, but I assumed he made it inside safely.

It was just Michael and me in the car as we drove down the highway of Ebon, the streetlights flashing in and out of my car. I kept checking the rearview mirror, but Michael never moved.

"Wanna listen to some radio?" I asked him as I reached for the volume knob, turning it up a smidgen.

Michael shrugged. "I don't care."

I sighed and clicked the knob inwards, shutting the radio off. "What's the matter, Michael?" I asked. "You've been acting strange."

Michael sighed and turned away from the window. He

looked at me in the rearview mirror as I glanced back and forth from him to the road. "You ever see somebody doing something and think you could do a better job than they could?"

I felt confused as I tried to figure out what Michael meant. "I mean, I guess, yeah. Why?"

Michael looked back out the window. "I feel like there's so many things I could do better than other people, you know? Like if only I had the chance."

"Well, then, just do it, you know?" I said, doing my best to offer some sort of encouragement.

"It's not that simple. I can't just do it."

"What do you mean?"

Michael waited a beat. I guessed he was trying to figure out whether or not he should tell me what he was thinking. "You know the Second Super—Tempest, some people call him?"

I began to get very hot, and I tightened my grip on the steering wheel. "Of course," I said, doing my best not to stammer. "Everybody knows Tempest."

"I feel like he's doing really shitty, you know? Like I could do so much better than he's doing."

I was taken aback. "Well," I began. I had to tread extremely lightly on this subject. "I don't think it's really that easy. I mean, at least it doesn't seem like it is."

Michael nodded. "Yeah, I agree, it's definitely not easy."

Damned straight.

"But I feel like if I were him, I'd be out there every night, saving people. If I were him, I'd stop every person from stealing, from killing, from abusing their family." Michael's voice was surprisingly not filled with anger, but filled with hope and wonder. "I'd be out there saving the world," he said. I looked back at him, and he was staring off into space, smiling, his eyes distant, thinking about the adventures he'd go on if he were Tempest.

"I'm sure he'll get to that eventually," I said. "I think he's probably trying to focus on Richter right now."

Michael nodded and sank back down into his seat. "Yeah, you're probably right. I just wish it'd get taken care of sooner, you know?"

I nodded and clicked the radio back on. I turned the volume to a really low level. "Me too, bud," I said. "More than you know," I whispered under my breath.

We drove without speaking, deep in our own thoughts, the radio playing the soundtrack to our drive. But then our soundtrack stopped as the radio went silent and a loud beeping noise was emitted by the speakers. The sudden loud noise caused both Michael and me to jump in our seats. A man's voice came from the speakers, filling the car.

"Attention, residents of Ebon and all towns in Fairview County. The federal government has issued a mandatory curfew beginning tomorrow night. No person should be out between ten o'clock at night and five thirty in the morning, unless it's in case of an emergency. No other exceptions. I am also announcing that the FBI is launching a full investigation into Tempest and the reports that he may be living in the area. If you are approached by a federal agent for questioning, please cooperate, as they are only here to help, and they have our safety and that of all United States citizens in mind. Their main base of operations will be at the Ebon Junior High School, and they will be acting in full cooperation with the Ebon Police Department. Should you have any more questions, please contact the EPD at 903-555-8584.

Thank you, and you will now be returned to your regularly scheduled programming."

The radio returned to playing music. Michael and I sat there in silence for a few moments, trying to process what we'd heard. It wasn't until I pulled into the parking lot in front of Michael's house that either of us said anything.

"Thanks for the ride," Michael said as he climbed out.

I was expecting him to say something about the curfew, and was relieved when he didn't. "No problem. Goodnight," I said before he shut the door.

I backed out of his driveway, and once his house was out of sight, I floored the gas pedal. My stomach sank and I began sweating. I hadn't used my powers, but still: the government was looking for me. And from the sound of what the president had said earlier, they weren't looking to be my friends.

"THIS IS NOT good," Dad said as we stood around the kitchen.

I was sitting on the counter, my legs swinging beneath me. I'd told Mom and Dad about the curfew and the government moving into town, searching for me.

"I thought they said they'd leave you alone as long as you didn't use your powers and interfere with them?" Mom asked.

"Yeah, that's what they said." I sighed in frustration. "How am I supposed to let this all blow over when they're out there looking for me? I can't defeat Richter like this!"

"I know, son. I know. We're going to have to see where this takes us. Everything will work out. Hey, who knows, maybe they do have some way of beating Richter. Then you wouldn't have to worry about anything at all!"

"Yeah, maybe," I mumbled. It all seemed like wishful thinking to me.

"Your father's right," Mom said. "Tempest and Richter have clashed in this city twice now. Maybe they're wanting to be ready for the next time it happens."

I pondered what she'd said for a moment. It made sense. If

they did have a way of defeating Richter, they'd go to the place where we had encountered each other multiple times.

"Maybe they're using me as bait," I said.

Mom sighed. "I don't like the idea of that. Not at all."

"Yeah, well, neither do I. But if it helps them defeat Richter so I don't have to do anything, that's fine by me."

Dad raised his hands, stopping Mom and me before we got into a fight. "The fact of the matter is that we're not one hundred percent sure of what we're dealing with here. Until things become more clear, your only option is to continue what you're doing and lie low."

I sighed. Yeah, I didn't want to become an enemy of the United States, but still, I wasn't confident of their ability to take down Richter. Not that I was all that confident of my own abilities either, but the real fact of the matter was that I was the only one who'd ever hurt Richter. Now I was hiding in my house, afraid of what the government might do to me.

An idea began to take shape in my head, but not one I would dare say out loud. My parents would kill me if they ever found out what I was thinking about doing.

"Well," I said as I pushed myself off the countertop. "I'm gonna go to bed now. It's been a long night."

Dad patted me on the back. "You're right, kid. Go get some rest. I'll stay up for a bit and keep an eye on the news, see if I can learn anything else."

I smiled at him and realized how thankful I was to have someone like my dad on my side. "Alright, sounds good."

I gave Mom a hug goodnight and then went upstairs to my room. The lights inside it were turned off, but I knew exactly where my bed was. I fell on top of it and lay there, waiting. I would have to wait a while before the coast was clear for me to sneak out.

I knew the smartest thing to do would be to do exactly what Dad wanted: to lie low. But when you're the only person who can stop a madman from destroying the world, lying low isn't an option.

*

I jumped out my bedroom window—sans Tempest outfit—and took off flying before I hit the ground. Flying was still such a weird, amazing sensation to me. One I doubted I'd ever get used to.

I slowed down once I got close to Ebon Middle School, flew a few thousand feet in the air to a spot above the school and hovered there, surveying the area. Using my eagle-like vision, I could see everything on the ground clearly. There were large generator lights spread out around the parking lot. Workers were unloading box after box of equipment from vans, and bringing them inside the middle school gym.

The middle school was right across the street from the high school, which I found amusing and ironic since the high school was where all of this had begun just a short time ago.

Large Humvees pulled into the school parking lot, and once they came to a stop, soldiers in dark clothing with assault rifles slung across their shoulders unloaded from the back. They joined the few soldiers who were already there and began to set up a perimeter. Most of them stayed in the front to help unload, some began setting up road barriers to keep people from entering the parking lot, while others began to spread out around the school, keeping watch over the back and sides.

One thing was clear: the government wasn't holding anything back.

I hovered over the school watching everything unfold. A pit began to grow in my stomach and I began to feel lightheaded. They looked as if they were preparing for a war, and I wasn't sure if I was friend or foe.

But I wasn't going to leave until I found out exactly what was going on.

CHAPTER 24

SEARCHING FOR ANSWERS

I FLEW DOWN CLOSER to try to get a look inside the gym, where the main base of operations was being set up. I landed behind one of the large generator lights, which had the letters DHS printed large on its side.

I poked my head around the corner and looked through the open doors that people were filing in and out of. Even though I was a good distance away, I could see what had to be hundreds of yards of wires being hooked up to various computers spread out across many individual desks and tables. The tables were set up in a series of squares; the largest was on the outside, and they got smaller and smaller. There was a gap that led to a podium in the center of the basketball court, where I assumed someone would stand to give mission updates and briefings.

Most people were still transporting items into the gym, so most of the laptops that had already been set up were left unattended. I knew that if I could get my hands on one of those, it was bound to contain loads of information pertaining to their mission. I couldn't run through the front door and grab one of the laptops, however. Yeah, I'd be moving fast enough, and it was dark enough that they probably wouldn't even notice the blur that ran past them, but the wind that would be caused by me running that fast would be sure to tip them off that something was up.

I decided to go in through a side door instead. I ran to the side of the middle school and pulled on one of the doors. Thankfully, it was unlocked. However, that meant that someone had to have gone through it, which meant that there could be guards in any of the classrooms down the long corridor that led to the gymnasium. Just to be safe, I decided not to run down the hallway at superspeed. I needed to be extra cautious, which meant crouching low to the ground and sneaking down the corridor keeping my head below the classroom windows and my senses on alert for any sign of soldiers patrolling the perimeter.

I began to sneak down the hallway, staying close to the wall. However, with every step I took, either my shoes squeaked, or my footsteps echoed around the empty hallway. They weren't that loud, but when you're sneaking around the makeshift top secret base of the Department of Homeland Security, they might as well have been as loud as gunshots.

Then I started thinking like a superhuman, and realized I could fly down the hallway. I lay down flat, face down on the floor. I then willed my body to float a few inches off the floor. I began to fly very slowly down the hallway, still sticking close to the walls. My eyes focused on the doors to the gym, and I concentrated on nothing else but reaching them.

I was so focused I almost didn't realize the door to the classroom in front of me had swung open. I stopped hard, my face an inch away from the wooden door. Two men walked out of the room, and I was frozen with fear. I had no idea what I would do if they turned around and saw me. I held my breath, not daring to make a sound.

Thankfully, the two men turned in the other direction and walked through the gym doors. The sound of the doors slamming echoed through the hallway like an explosion.

I let out the breath I'd been holding. I'd never felt so relieved. I decided that I should probably pick up the pace a little. Even though I wanted answers, I would be glad when it finally came time to get out of there.

I reached the doors at the end of the hallway and lowered myself to the ground. I crouched up against the door and slowly slid my body upwards, stopping as soon as the smallest sliver of the room came into view.

From this angle, I could tell that most of the people were toward the front of the room, as they'd finished setting up the back of the room. That meant they were almost through though, which meant I was running out of time.

In the back corner sat an unattended laptop that was turned on and set up. It was the farthest away from anyone, and the closest to me, so snatching that one would be my best bet.

I closed my eyes and took a deep breath, trying to calm my nerves. I counted to three, and then ran as fast as I could through the double gym doors. I made a beeline for the laptop, running as fast as I could. I looked to my right and caught a look at the government workers, who seemed to be frozen in time. All of them were either making their way outside, or getting computers and televisions set up, so nobody was paying any attention to the back of the room. No one would see a blur run in and out, or notice the missing laptop.

I grabbed the computer, turned around, and ran back

out the doors that I had come in through. I slowed down and came to a stop in the middle of the hallway, then snuck back over to the double doors that led to the gym and sat down next to them. I wanted to be close by so that if I heard or saw anyone making their way to the back, I'd be able to see them in time and get the laptop back before they noticed, hopefully without them noticing me.

I got to work. I opened the documents folder of the laptop and was met with a sea of files that would take forever to go through. I clicked on the search bar and entered *Tempest*. I was surprised at how few files popped up, but then again, I'd done a pretty good job of covering my tracks.

I opened a file called *Tempest Possible Locations 7_15_15 Revision*. When the file opened, there were only the names of a few towns—Ebon, Indiana, right at the top, of course. There were no specific names, though, which was good for me. They had an idea of what town I lived in, nothing more.

I exited out of the file, then checked to make sure no one was going to the back of the gym, but everyone was still unloading and setting up. I knew it was only a matter of time, though, so I had to work fast.

I searched for *Richter* next, and tons of files popped up. One that caught my eye was called *Richter Known Locations*. I double-clicked on it, and when it opened, I couldn't help but smile. It was a list of exact known hideouts of Richter. The one at the top was the Statue of Liberty, one of the few landmarks left standing in New York City. The rest of the locations on the list were places like the Taj Mahal Hotel, the Eiffel Tower, the Burj Khalifa, and a couple of other really luxurious and exotic places.

I exited the file and was about to open one called *Richter*

Known Associates 6_30_15, but approaching footsteps broke my concentration. I looked through the window and saw a lady with black hair pulled back in a ponytail and her head buried in a tablet approaching the back of the room. I panicked. I got up, and after double-checking to be sure that she had her attention glued to her tablet, I ran through the door as fast as I could, put the laptop back, ran back through the doors, and came to a stop in the hallway.

I ducked into one of the classrooms and crouched down behind the door. I felt the euphoric sensation of almost getting caught, but not, as I tried to catch my breath.

After a couple of minutes of sitting there, once my nerves had calmed down, I began to listen closely. I wanted to see if I could hear anyone discussing what they were doing here, so I could get more of an idea of what exactly was going on. The result of my listening was eerie, though. Nobody was saying a word. The only sounds were those of shuffling feet and clicking keys.

I listened for a few more minutes, hoping that someone would get bored and let something slip about *anything.* But there was nothing. That is, until someone cleared their voice and began to shout. The sudden noise almost made me jump, but I recovered quickly and began to listen as carefully as I could.

"Everyone pay attention," a woman shouted. All other sounds stopped at once as everybody listened closely, myself included. "If your workstation is set up, I want you to go to it immediately. If it is still being set up, once I am done speaking you have five minutes to get it finished and ready to go." The woman paused for a few moments, letting everyone acknowledge what she'd said. "Now, many of you know why we're here, but you don't know the specifics. I will tell you our main mission goals, and then your commanding officer will tell you the specifics of what he or she wants you to do. Understood?"

Everybody in the room shouted "Understood!" in unison. I brought my hands to my ears and pulled back on my listening as my ears rang in pain from the noise. I quickly expanded my listening reach back, though, not wanting to miss a thing.

"We believe that Ebon is the most likely candidate for the town that Tempest is hiding in. There are a few other possibilities, and smaller teams have been deployed to scout those locations. However, all of you here are working at the largest branch of this operation. If you're here, it's because I wanted you here. It's because you're the best at what you do. And I expect nothing less than excellence. There are many lives on the line here, and many have been lost already. The sooner we take down the superhuman menace, the sooner the world can return to normal.

"Tempest is our primary target. You are to find him and capture him. This will not be an easy task, but given what we've learned from studying Richter and now Tempest, we believe that Tempest is weaker than Richter. Therefore, tactics that did not prove useful on Richter may work on Tempest. Some of you are here to figure out which ones will work best, while others are here to execute the missions. It's important that we bring Tempest in alive. We must study him in order to find out what weaknesses these bastard Supers have, so that we can put an end to them. We only may get one shot at this, so I will accept no failures. Every failure is a life lost due to one of Richter's rampages, or a battle between him and Tempest."

I heard someone's sleeve brush against the body of their shirt as—I assumed—they raised their hand.

"Yes?" the woman asked.

"Yes, Agent Loren, I was wondering why we're treating Tempest as the enemy? It seems like he just wants to help."

"This isn't a goddamned think tank. You don't think we've thought through this shit? When has a Super ever done good? Billions of dollars in damage, cities destroyed, an unfathomable number of lives lost. The numbers speak for themselves. If we want peace in this world, the Supers must be eradicated."

I listened to every word she said, enthralled and terrified. But something tore me from Agent Loren's briefing. My range of listening contracted as I realized that the doorknob above me had turned, and the door was swinging open. I looked up and came eye to eye with two soldiers. Their guns were drawn and pointed right at me.

CHAPTER 25
A FEW QUESTIONS

I WAS SITTING AT a desk in the front row of the classroom for probably the first time ever. My hands lay handcuffed on the desk while two guards stood in front of the teacher's desk, the safeties on their guns off. Moonlight filtered through the window of the classroom, giving everything an ethereal glow. It was probably really dark to most people, the moonlight not offering much illumination. I, on the other hand, thanks to my powers, could see everything crystal clear. Not as if it was daylight, but everything was just...*clear.* Nothing was hidden, not even the slight look of worry the soldier on the right had, no matter how hard he tried to hide it.

The door opened, and in walked a man in his late twenties or early thirties. He walked over and stood between the two guards, and leaned up against the teacher's desk. He examined me for a moment before pushing himself off the desk. He walked over to me and extended his hand.

"Hello, my name is Agent York," he said, charm and charisma oozing from his every word. He was holding out his hand as if he expected me to shake it.

I raised my two cuffed hands. "Sorry, I can't shake your hand in these cuffs."

Agent York scoffed. "Oh, please, it's not like they're behind your back. Still—" He gestured to one of the guards and pointed at my restrained hands. "I'll still remove them, if to do nothing more than humor you."

The soldier uncuffed my hands, and I rubbed my wrists, acting as if they hurt, even though I felt no pain. I shook Agent York's hand. "A pleasure to meet you," I said with a knowing smile.

York smiled, dimples appearing on his face as he did so. "And your name is?"

I hesitated for a moment, then decided that it would probably be best to give them my real name. They would be able to find out as soon as I left whether I was lying or not by doing a search in one of their many databases. Besides, they didn't have even the slightest idea who Tempest was. "My name is Kane Andrews."

York cocked his head to the side and looked up toward the ceiling. He leaned back onto the teacher's desk and crossed his arms. "Hmm. Kane. That's an interesting name."

I let out a sigh, over-exaggerating to let him think I was getting impatient. Even though, really, I was slightly freaking out on the inside.

Agent York smirked. "Getting impatient, I see? Well, there's no reason to keep you here much longer. I just have a few questions for you."

"Then I can leave?" I asked.

"If you answer them correctly."

I didn't like the sound of that. "Can I ask you one?"

"Sure, why not. We're all friends here."

I wasn't so sure about that, but I ignored his comment for the time being. "Who exactly are you?"

"Well, we're the Department of Homeland Security," he said, gesturing to the DHS lettering over the right breast of his black jacket.

"No," I said. "Who are *you*? Are you in charge here or something?"

Agent York nodded. "Yes, I run this show."

I gave him a look like I was impressed, but really, I knew it was all bullshit. Agent Loren was the real person in charge. It took me a minute to figure out why she wasn't the one questioning me. I then realized that of course they wouldn't want to send in the person in charge. If I was a bad guy, I'd know who to target. Agent York was like a taste-tester: he had to make sure everything was good, so if something went wrong, he'd be the one taken out, not the person in charge. It made sense, although I did find it slightly morbid.

"Can I get on with my questions now?" he asked.

I leaned back in my chair and crossed my arms. "Please," I said, my confidence growing. They were trying to play me, but little did they know that I was already figuring their game out.

"What are you doing in here, Kane?" Agent York asked, giving me a quizzical, almost over-the-top look.

"Well, I was hanging out with some buddies of mine when we drove by here and saw what was going on. We started betting one another to see who had guts enough to try to sneak in and back out without getting caught. Finally I decided that the bets were high enough for me to risk sneaking in, and, well—" I gestured toward the two soldiers standing on either side of York. "It looks like I owe my buddies seventy-five bucks."

Agent York chuckled and shook his head. "Teenagers," he said. "They'll do the stupidest things for a few bucks."

I shrugged. "What can I say?"

"How about you tell me if you know anything about Tempest?" Agent York suggested. "I mean, you had to have heard something, right? You look like you're a popular kid. You know some people. Surely you've heard rumors?"

I looked away from York. My stomach twisted, but I maintained a straight face. "Listen," I began, turning back to him. "Pretty much all of us around here keep quiet about that Tempest guy. Dude's a bad omen. A buddy of mine mentioned him and the next day his car was stolen." I winced. I was laying it on a little thick, and told myself to back down a little. It felt so good, knowing something that they didn't know I knew. Feeling like I was the one in control of the situation, while they still thought they were.

"So you're saying you don't know anything?" Agent York pressed me for answers.

I shook my head. "Nope. Just a guy looking for a thrill, making a couple bucks off my friends, and coming out with a good story in the end."

Agent York smirked. "Well, Kane, I'm sure your buddies will love to hear this one."

"Does that mean I'm free to go?" I asked.

York nodded. "Yes, as long as you promise to stay out of our way. And if you hear anything at all about Tempest"— he reached into his jacket pocket and pulled out a business card—"you give me a call."

I took the business card from him and looked it over. It had *Agent York* printed on the front in italic letters. I flipped it over; on the back was his phone number. That was it. Nothing more, nothing less.

I shoved it in my pocket and stood up from my desk. I extended my hand to Agent York and smiled. "Thank you," I said as he shook my hand. "And I'm really sorry if I caused any trouble."

"Of course, Kane." He gestured to the soldier on his right. "This gentleman will escort you off the premises."

"Thank you again," I said as I turned and walked out of the room. The soldier followed close behind before catching up to me and walking with me side by side. He said nothing as we exited the building, which was good, because I was listening to what was going on in the classroom.

"Should we follow him?" the soldier who was still in there asked.

There was a pause before Agent York sighed. "No, not yet. We were expecting some punk kids to come see what was going on. It's a small town, middle of summer, nothing to do. Kids get bored. Besides, we're still getting set up around here. We can't spare the manpower until all the agents coming in arrive tomorrow. I'll have one of our technicians run his name through the database to make sure nothing pops up. I want you to tell your men to keep an eye out for this kid, though. If we catch him doing anything suspicious, I want people watching him like a hawk."

"Yes, sir," the soldier said. The two men exited the room, ending the conversation.

I returned my attention to my surroundings, and I noticed we had reached the end of the parking lot. "My friends are parked across the street," I said, pointing to the almost-filled parking lot of the high school. "Late night volunteering at the shelter," I added.

The soldier shrugged, not caring about my excuse. "Just get out of here, and stay out. We could've accidentally killed you tonight."

"I'll keep that in mind."

With that, I jogged across the road and into the parking lot. I ran around to the back of the high school, where it was pitch black and no one was around to see me. After scanning the area a couple more times to be sure the coast was clear, I launched myself into the air and flew home.

CHAPTER 26

TO THE STARS

I PICKED UP THE tractor and launched it into the air with ease. I didn't send it too high since I didn't want anyone to see a tractor flying through the air and wonder what was going on. Even though I was in a clearing I'd found deep in the woods behind my house, I still wanted to play it safe.

I flew up beneath the tractor and brought it safely to the ground. Once it touched down, I picked it up, threw it, and caught it again, bringing it down as easily as I could. It wasn't the most glamorous or useful form of training, but it was better than nothing. I couldn't just sit around and do nothing; I had to try to improve in any way I could to be ready the next time I faced Richter. Which was something that I was going to have to do fast. I had to find Richter and defeat him before Homeland Security found me and experimented on me. I had to defeat Richter, if not for anybody's sake but my own.

After playing catch with the tractor for a little while, I decided to work on my flight. I stood in the middle of the clearing and closed my eyes. I took a few deep breaths and became aware of every little sound around me. The insects singing, the birds chirping, and the wind blowing through the trees, causing their leaves to whisper in harmony.

It all disappeared as I launched myself into the air at super-speed, breaking the sound barrier before I reached the tops of the trees. My ears popped, and the wind whipped my hair back. I was somehow able to keep my eyes open, but they didn't fill with tears from the wind. Maybe it had something to do with the fact that I was making them glow, but I wasn't certain.

I came to a stop at around fifteen thousand feet and looked at the world beneath me. I could see far off into the distance. I could see everything on the horizon clearly, thanks to my enhanced vision. I would've been able to see much past the horizon but couldn't because of the curve of the Earth.

I turned my eyes upward and could see a plane flying above me at about thirty thousand feet. That's when the question popped into my head, one that I couldn't help but answer as soon as I'd asked it.

How high can I go?

I smirked to myself. *This'll be fun,* I thought, right before I flew upward as fast as I could. The earth below me shot away like a bullet. I flew up and up, faster and faster. The sky began to turn from blue to black as I began to leave the atmosphere.

Suddenly, all the wind that had been blowing in my face just moments before stopped. I freaked out for a split second, thinking I'd stopped flying. When I looked down, though, I could see that the ground was still getting farther and farther away.

I realized I'd reached the upper levels of the atmosphere, where there was no wind resistance. I remembered something I'd learned when I was a kid, obsessed with space and being an astronaut, like most kids are at some point. When a space shuttle is going up to the International Space Station, it reaches speeds of seventeen thousand miles per hour once it leaves the Earth's lower atmosphere, thanks to it not having to fly against the wind resistance, and because gravity is getting lower and lower.

Which meant that even though I thought I was going as fast as I could, once I began to leave the Earth's atmosphere and venture into low orbit, I began to go even faster. It was like somebody had strapped rockets onto me. I began to fly so fast I began to wonder if I'd be able to stop.

That thought terrified me and I began to slow down. I went slower and slower until I came to a stop.

I began to examine my surroundings, and my breath was taken away. The sky was black and endless, like an infinite void. I realized that it wasn't the sky anymore; it was space.

I turned around and my whole body went weak as I looked upon the Earth below me. It stretched as far as the eye could see on either side of me. It was bright and blue, with white clouds spread over much of the green United States. I soaked in the unbelievable sight. I wanted to say something for some reason, but the words were escaping me.

Then I found them. "How the hell have I not suffocated or frozen?"

I tried breathing in and out a couple of times, but I couldn't get any air in. I began to panic, the feeling of not being able to breathe being a terrible one. I realized then that I wasn't actually suffocating. My regenerative powers were some-how still keeping me alive, even though I wasn't breathing at all. Still, I began to feel weak, the same as I had when Richter threw me into the mountain. Once I got out of my hole and began breathing clean, fresh air, I regenerated much quicker. I suspected that while I could survive up here, I would fare much better if I was in an environment with oxygen.

I also felt warm, despite the fact that the temperature was definitely well below freezing. I wanted to know how and why all these things were possible. Not knowing how I could do such spectacular things really annoyed me. I was beginning to get used to my powers, and now I was simply curious as to how they all worked.

But that would have to wait until Richter had been taken care of and I was safe from the government.

After admiring the view and being alone with my thoughts for a few more moments, I decided it was time to return to the Earth. The feeling of not breathing was an unnerving one, one I doubted I would ever get used to, and I was beginning to feel weak. I began to fly toward the ground, eager to be breathing fresh air once again.

I admired the amazing view that surrounded me as I began to fly back home at a much slower pace than I had taken on my way up. It was all so beautiful. I know the word *beautiful* is thrown around so much that to most people, the meaning behind it is lost. Same thing goes for the word *awesome*. But the flight down was literally awe-inspiring, and filled with beauty.

I looked north, and could see Indianapolis in the distance. It was about a hundred miles away from Ebon, but from my height with my eyesight, I could see it as clear as day.

Something flying above the city caught my eye. I began to slow my descent, and that was when I realized that the object above the city wasn't flying, it was hovering.

I recognized the glowing eyes and evil grin. It was Richter, and he was staring right at me. Even though he was a hundred miles away, I knew he was watching me, and he knew I was watching him. I stared at him for a few moments, waiting for him to do something.

After a minute, he moved. He flew straight down, into the streets of Indianapolis.

As soon as he moved, so did I, aiming directly for him.

It was time for me to put an end to Richter once and for all.

CHAPTER 27

RICHTER'S GAME

I FLEW TOWARD INDIANAPOLIS and reached the city limits in a matter of seconds. I flew to where I had seen Richter last, above some of the skyscrapers downtown. I flew down to street level, and was struck by how eerily quiet things were.

Most people had fled the city and were in shelters in various parts of the state, like the one in Ebon High School. It was a weird disconnect, being in such a large city that was usually bustling with activity, yet it was completely silent, save for the wind blowing some papers and other garbage across the ground.

I scanned the surroundings, searching for Richter. There was no sign of him anywhere.

"How are you today, *Tempest*?" His mocking voice echoed loudly around the empty city streets.

It sounded louder to my right, however, and I ran over there in a split second, hoping I'd be able to catch him before he moved.

I was too late, as evidenced by the next round of insults that seemed to come from the other end of the street.

"Too slow, *Tempest*." Every time he said my name, it was like an insult. As if the words were poison in his mouth, and he had to spit them out before they killed him. "Too *inferior*."

I ran to the other side of the street as fast as I could, hoping to prove him wrong. I was still too slow, though; as I reached the other side, I saw a blur disappear through the broken window of one of the nearby skyscrapers.

I launched into the air and flew through the window. I found myself inside a dark office building. Cubicles lined the room as far as the eye could see.

Richter flew past me in a blur, hitting me hard to the floor as he flew out the broken window the two of us had just come through.

I pushed myself up off the ground with a grunt. I looked out of the building and could see Richter in the building across the street, standing behind an unbroken window, waving at me. A sly, mocking smile crept across his face.

I felt rage and frustration boil up inside me. I launched out of the building and flew across the street as fast as I could. I didn't slow down as I reached the window, but right before I burst through it, Richter disappeared in a blur.

The window shattered and I landed on the floor, glass raining down around me. I tried my best not to yell in frustration, not wanting to show Richter any sign that he was winning, even though he most definitely already knew he was. I wasn't giving up, though. Not when the government wanted to experiment on me to figure out how to defeat him.

I turned and jumped out of the building, and fell several stories. I landed on the ground with a hard thud. "Why don't you come out here and stop running like a child!" I shouted, my voice carrying throughout the empty streets. It was so loud, I even surprised myself.

"Oh, Tempest. Everyone says when they're older that they wish they could be a kid again! I may be acting like a child, but children have *fun*. And you've gotta admit—" Richter paused. The next words weren't an echo in the street, but a whisper in my ear. "*This is fun.*"

Richter struck me in the back, sending me flying into a nearby car. The metal crushed beneath the force of my momentum. I pushed myself up off the car as fast as I could and landed on my feet, ready for a fight.

Another blow came from my left, sending me flying down the street and skidding across the asphalt. I felt my Tempest suit tear from the friction, and my skin burned as it began to rub away. I pushed my hands down to stop myself and stood up. I felt a coolness on my hands and back as my flesh and skin began to quickly heal.

Richter's next move was a mistake, as he began to get cocky. He thought he could run directly at me, and was going to try and get in a punch to my face.

I saw his blur coming and ducked down just in time, extending my arm, clotheslining him. He let out a grunt in pain and fright and went tumbling through two cars before coming to a stop on a third.

My arm healed itself as I ran to where he was lying on the car. This time he was too slow, and I picked him up by his blue and white striped shirt and threw him through the skyscraper to my right.

Richter went flying through the wall, and I was close behind. I flew through the holes he created in the building before he began to fall to the ground. He slid across it, breaking it up into a deep trench. He finally came to a stop in the street on the other side of the building.

I was on top of him as soon as he stopped, and punched him a few more times in the face, letting out all my rage and frustration, while at the same time feeling euphoric from the fact that I was winning.

Except I wasn't.

He grabbed my fist before I could punch him again and knocked it away, causing my fist to embed in the ground next to his head. He let out a yell as he punched my trapped arm, causing it to break clean in half.

I yelled in pain as the bone and flesh began to stitch itself back together. Even though it only took a few seconds before I was fine again, that was more than enough time for Richter.

He jumped on top of me, taking me to the ground. He hit me a couple of times in the face so hard that it sent shock-waves through the street. "You're going to pay for that!" he yelled as loud as he could. So loud that windows in the buildings around us shattered and glass began to rain down on us.

Richter grabbed me and picked me up. He launched into the air, and before I could even react, he'd flown a hundred miles away.

He changed his course, and suddenly the two of us were flying straight down. I turned my head just in time to see that we were flying straight toward the roof of Ebon High School, with no sign of slowing down.

We exploded through the roof of the gymnasium, rubble flying everywhere. The terrified screams of innocent people reached my ears. Richter and I crashed into the ground, causing a large crater to appear. The screams of terror turned to sickening screams of pain as rubble from the roof fell on top of the people who'd cried out.

Richter pushed himself off me and hovered above my body. Dust filled the air, dancing in the beams of sunlight that filtered in through the open ceiling. I couldn't move. Once again, my spine had been severed and I was paralyzed. I could feel it cracking and moving as my body worked to repair itself.

Even if I'd had the ability to move, I wouldn't have been able to. I would have been paralyzed by shock.

Because lying just a few feet away from me was a dead body. He had been crushed by a large piece of the gymnasium roof. His eyes were open and they stared at me, filled with shock.

I felt my fingers move. I had control of my body again. I didn't turn to attack Richter, however. I continued to lie there. I let out a scream as tears began to fall from my eyes.

Because it wasn't just anybody who'd died and was lying inches away from me.

It was Michael.

I got up. I had to help him. I had to get him to a hospital, even though a little voice in my head told me it was too late.

I was pushed back to the ground. Richter had his hand on my head and was forcing me to look into Michael's dead eyes.

"Look at him, *Tempest*," he said. "Look at him!"

I thought I was going to throw up. "Michael, no. No, Michael, no," I whispered.

"He's dead because of you."

"No," I said.

"Yes, *Tempest*."

"NO!" I shouted. I tried to fight against Richter, but his grip was too tight, and growing tighter by the second.

"Yes! This is what happens when you don't play along. This is what happens when you're out of your league." Richter got down next to my face. "How does it feel, Tempest? How does it feel to be the bad guy?"

I didn't respond. I couldn't.

Richter let go of me. "Think about it, Tempest. Then let's see how well you play next time." With that, he flew up and out through the hole we'd created in the ceiling.

I got up from the ground and picked up the rubble that was on top of Michael. I threw it into the air, out the hole in the ceiling. Then I picked up Michael's lifeless body in my arms and ran out of the school as fast as I could.

I reached the hospital in less than a second. I found myself standing in the Emergency Room screaming, "SOMEBODY HELP ME!"

Doctors and nurses came running to see what was going on. They all froze in fear when they saw who was standing there.

So instead, I ran to them. They all let out a gasp as I suddenly appeared in front of one of the doctors, a tall woman with graying hair.

"Please," I pleaded as I handed Michael over to her. "Please."

But deep down, I knew that I was already too late.

CHAPTER 28

CROSSROADS

I LANDED HARD IN the clearing I'd found deep within the woods. I pulled back my mask, letting it hang behind me like the hood portion of a hoodie. I fell to my knees and let out a frustrated scream. I screamed so loud, I felt my throat begin to tear and repair itself. Birds flew away and other wildlife ran in fear.

I fell to the ground. My whole body felt numb, and my mind was lethargic. I couldn't think about anything. All I could do was feel. Angry, frustrated, sad, full of hate. Those emotions coursed through me. They were paralyzing.

I couldn't believe it. Richter had defeated me yet again, and at the cost of the life of my best friend. Precious Michael. Such a sweet person. Always overshadowed in our circle of friends by Drew, yet always appreciated. I felt tears begin to form in my eyes. I lay on the ground, the grass pressing against my face. The tears fell and watered the grass with their salty poison.

But the longer I lay there, the more my attention turned to one emotion in particular: rage. My body began to shake, the ferocity of the emotion coursing through my body like a roaring river.

I jumped up from the ground and with a yell charged into a tree at the edge of the clearing. The tree thundered and splintered with a loud crack. It fell to the ground with a satisfying thud, and somehow, I felt a little bit better.

I wound up for another swing and hit the tree to my left as hard as I could. It, too, fell to the ground, relieving some of my frustration as it fell.

I was about to take another tree out as my frustration and rage began to turn to glee, but something made me stop. A feeling in my gut that I couldn't quite ignore. A feeling that told me what I was doing was wrong.

I fell back to the ground and looked at the two trees I'd killed. I don't know why, but I felt guilty. Not exactly because I'd knocked down two trees, but because I felt as if I'd fallen to Richter's level. Richter was the one who'd gone down the path of destruction, not me. I couldn't bring myself down to his level.

Still, even though I didn't agree with him, even though I despised what he was doing, and knew it was wrong, I understood why. And that terrified me.

If I felt the way I was feeling after Michael's death, I could only imagine how it must've felt for Richter after his entire family had been slaughtered. Suddenly, things began to make a lot more sense.

I found myself at a crossroads. The same crossroads I was sure that Richter had found himself at.

That day, in that clearing, was when I chose the path I would go down. I wouldn't go down the one Richter had chosen. His family had died because he was a destructive, homicidal maniac, and once they were dead, Richter had gotten even worse. He'd killed and destroyed even more. His family had died in vain.

I promised myself that Michael's death wouldn't be in vain. I wasn't going to cause any more pain or destruction. I stood up and took in a deep breath. I remembered what Michael had said a few days ago as I drove him home from the party. He'd said that he wished he could be Tempest—that he could be *me*. That he would do a better job, and he'd get things done.

I promised myself that I would be the person that Michael had wanted to be. The *hero* he'd wanted to be.

But just because I'd resolved to *be* a hero didn't mean I was one yet. I had a long way to go. But that day in the clearing, I chose my path on the crossroads.

I chose Michael's path.

I chose the path of the hero.

MICHAEL'S FUNERAL WAS a few days later. I sat in the third row of chairs at the funeral home, staring at the closed casket. I imagined Michael lying inside of it, his eyes closed in an eternal sleep. I wished it would have been an open casket funeral, though. I would've loved to see Michael's face one last time, so my last memory of him would be of him looking peaceful. Now for the rest of my life, my last memory of him would be how terrified he had looked as the debris crushed him. Debris that was there because I couldn't defeat Richter.

Macy's hand tightened around mine, breaking me from my train of thought. I looked to my right where she was sitting, and her sad eyes looked up at me. She said nothing, but her face said what wasn't spoken. It was filled with sorrow, but she tried to force a smile in order to cheer me up.

It made me fall in love with her that much more, but at the same time, it made me feel even more guilty. I'd resolved that I wouldn't let Michael's death be in vain; that it would mean something. That helped with the guilt factor a lot. But seeing all the sorrow and pain in the packed funeral home was suffocating. I felt like I'd go crazy if I had to see one more sad face, or hear one more person try to hide their sobbing.

I looked to my left at Drew, who was sitting next to me. He was staring straight forward, and of all things, he looked angry. I wanted to ask him what he was thinking, but knew it'd be inappropriate.

The funeral lasted another twenty minutes, and once it was over with, everybody began to pile into their cars to drive to the graveside. Drew, Macy, and I decided to ride together in my car, even though Drew and I had ridden to the funeral with our parents, and Macy with her sister.

We sat in the car in silence, following the endless parade of cars as I drove us to the cemetery.

Finally, Drew said something. "Does this feel real to you guys?"

Macy shook her head. "Not at all."

I said nothing. This all was too real for me.

"So many people dead," Macy said. "All thanks to Richter. I never thought Michael would be one of them."

Drew fumed with anger in the backseat. "Not just thanks to him, thanks to Tempest, too."

"Tempest was only trying to help. You can't blame him," Macy said.

She was half right, half wrong. I was only trying to help, but I did deserve the blame.

"Oh, shut up, Macy. You're just blinded because Tempest made his big debut saving your ass. He might have saved you, but he also killed Michael. Just because the scales are balanced doesn't mean we have to let him off."

Macy scoffed. "He didn't go out of his way to kill Michael.

It was Richter. He's the one you should blame. He's the one you should get mad at, not me."

Drew let out a condescending snort. "You don't get it. But I don't expect you to. You don't understand. You only knew Michael for a couple of months. Kane and I have known him our whole lives. Don't act like you were his best friend."

Macy said nothing in response. She just turned her head to look out the window, trying to hide the tears that were now flowing. Drew's words had cut her deep. I looked in the rearview mirror and prepared to shoot Drew a look that said, *What the hell?!* but he, too, had his attention focused on the trees that passed us by as we drove out of Ebon.

I sighed and turned my attention back to the road. I didn't have the mental stamina to try to even begin to process the fight Drew and Macy had just gotten into. I couldn't bring myself to do it. I wanted to forget it and pretend it had never happened. But I couldn't. The words exchanged between the two of them would haunt me for a good long while.

*

I sat on the living room couch, staring at the ceiling. Mom, Dad, and I had just gotten back from the funeral, so we were all still processing everything. Mom and Dad had tried to talk to me about what had happened a few times, but I wasn't ready to talk about it, and they understood. They didn't push me, and for that I was thankful.

I was trying to think about Michael, to remember some of the good times the two of us had had in order to cheer myself up. But no matter how hard I tried not to, all I could think about was the argument between Drew and Macy. And, in particular, one thing that Drew had said. He'd spoken about all the lives lost thanks to Richter. My mind couldn't help but linger on that thought.

There were so many Michaels in the world, dead because of Richter. So many Drews and Macys, torn apart inside because of the death of a loved one. Not only that, but friendships ripping at the seams as well. I couldn't imagine how his parents and other family members felt.

So much pain and suffering, all because of Richter. I couldn't even begin to imagine how many people had had to go through what we were going through because of Richter. Because of his grief and madness.

That's when it came to me. I felt passion for this new resolve burn inside of me. I realized that I had to defeat Richter, not just to protect my family, not to save myself from the government, and not because I was the only one who actually had a chance to win. No, I had to stop Richter for the sake of all the Michaels, Macys, Drews, and Kanes of the world. I had to stop all the pain and suffering he was causing, and I didn't realize that until I felt the pain and suffering myself.

The best way to end the pain and suffering I felt, and to keep anyone else from feeling the same way, was by providing closure. And the only way that would happen was by defeating Richter.

I knew that I couldn't do it alone. I could have all the motivation in the world, but that didn't change the fact that Richter was better at using his powers. But if I had the right people on my side, helping me, I knew I could do it.

I took a deep breath and did my best to calm myself. I was brimming with excitement, because for the first time, I felt that defeating Richter was a real possibility.

But that was only if I could get Agent Loren and the rest of the U.S. government on my side.

CHAPTER 30

THE LION'S DEN

MOM SQUEEZED ME tight, not wanting to let me go. "Please, Kane, please be safe," she whispered into my ear.

I squeezed her back. "Don't worry, Mom. I'm pretty tough."

She chuckled and then released me from her hug.

I turned to Dad, and his face was filled with pride for me. I smiled at him and gave him a hug. I don't know why it felt as if we were saying goodbye. I had every intention of returning home to them. I guessed that being surrounded by death for so long had made me a little bit more thankful, made me cherish every moment.

I pushed away from Dad. "Alright," I began. "I gotta go. Keep an eye on the news," I said with a smile. "You just might see me."

"Your father and I are so proud of you," Mom said, her face glowing.

I didn't know why, but I wanted to cry. I held back the tears, though. This wasn't the time for tears. It was time for me to be Tempest, not Kane.

"Thanks," I said. "I'll see you later, I guess."

"See you later," Dad said.

I turned and walked out the door. I pulled the headpiece of my Tempest suit over my face, and made my eyes glow. I fought the urge to turn around and take one last glance at Mom and Dad.

You can see them when you come home, I told myself.

I rocketed into the air and began flying to Ebon Middle School. It was time for me to pay Agent Loren and Homeland Security a visit.

*

I hovered above the middle school. I looked down upon it and took a deep breath, trying to calm my nerves. There was no time to stand—or float—around, though, so I descended to the ground. It was now or never.

My feet touched the ground, and I began walking to the gym. I focused my glowing eyes on the twin gymnasium doors.

The five soldiers guarding the doors noticed me approaching and scrambled to get their guns ready and aimed at me.

"Freeze!" one of them shouted.

I ignored his orders and continued walking toward the door. I was thirty feet away, and my heart was beating fast.

"Don't you move!" they shouted again.

One of the others began whispering something into his radio.

Suddenly, when I was only fifteen feet away, the doors burst open, and out came Agent York, the guy who'd interrogated me in the classroom.

I stopped when I saw him.

"Tempest," he said. "What brings you around here?" His

charm and charisma were distracting. I could tell why he was the one they'd chosen to be the fake leader of this operation.

"I'm here to speak to the one in charge," I said. I altered my voice by vibrating my vocal cords, a trick I'd learned after the situation in Texas.

York raised his hands and smiled. "You're looking at him."

I scoffed. "I'm sorry, I should say that I would like to speak to the *woman* in charge. Agent Loren, I believe?"

Shock crossed all of the soldiers' faces, but no one looked more shocked than Agent York. After all, his job was to keep Agent Loren a secret.

"I-uh-I," he stammered, unable to find the words.

"Go get her for me, please," I said, interrupting him.

Agent York shut his mouth and walked back inside, clearly embarrassed.

Nobody said a word while we waited for Agent York to return, with Agent Loren hopefully in tow. I watched the door while the soldiers watched me, guns aimed and ready to fire.

After a few more moments, the door opened and out walked Agent Loren, with York following close behind. He looked as if he were a puppy that had just been kicked. She looked very upset.

"Hello, Agent Loren," I said when she walked out.

"Tempest," she said. "How do you know who I am?"

"Agent York is a good actor, but he comes off a little green. It was a bit obvious."

"That still doesn't explain how you know my name, or Agent York's for that matter," she said, insistent.

"That's not relevant," I said. "I've come to have a discussion with you."

"Unless you've come to turn yourself in, I'm not interested in a discussion," she said.

"I think you'll want to hear my proposition. That is, unless you want to continue to allow Richter to terrorize the world."

Now she looked intrigued. She crossed her arms and nodded. "I'm listening."

I smiled. It was going better than I'd expected so far. "I've tried on a few occasions to defeat Richter myself."

"I'm aware," Loren said. She gestured her head toward the high school across the street. "I've seen the results myself."

I pushed down the anger and frustration that rose up inside of me. To this woman, I was still the enemy. I needed to remind myself of that, and do what I could to show her I was not. "Yes, my attempts have been less than successful. However, I'm the only one who's ever been able to do any kind of damage to Richter." I paused for a moment, to let that fact sink in. "You want Richter gone, as do I. We share those goals. But you cannot take him on your own, and neither can I. However, if we work together, I believe we can take him down. And hopefully, eventually, things will return to normal."

Agent Loren mulled over what I'd said for a moment before speaking. "How can I trust you, Tempest? How do I know you're not trying to spy on us? Taking us down from the inside?"

"Agent Loren, if I wanted to take you down, I would've done so the minute your trucks pulled up here. And I wouldn't have to do it from the inside. I could kill all of you here in the blink of an eye if I wanted to. But I don't. All I want to do is see Richter ended. Eventually, I'll probably be able to do that on my own, without you. But that will take a while, and a lot of lives will be lost in the meantime. I'm giving you the chance to end this, and end this now, before anyone else has to die." I let her process what I was saying. "With or without you," I said after a few moments. "I will take Richter down. I can just do it a lot sooner if I have you and your people on my side."

Agent Loren sighed. "What other choice do we have?" she asked. "It's clear we were wrong about possibly being able to take you into custody ourselves."

"You're right about that. But, hey, I understand. You were desperate. But now you don't have to be." I walked over to her, the soldiers tensing up as I did so, but she waved her hand and they relaxed. I extended my hand. "Truce?"

She looked at my hand for a moment, thinking about it. Finally, she grabbed it in a firm grasp and shook. "Truce."

CHAPTER 31

A PLAN

"GIVEN THE INFORMATION provided to us by Tempest regarding his regenerative powers, we think we may have a way to stop Richter," Dr. Reynolds, the lead scientist of the mission, said.

Agent Loren, Agent York, Dr. Reynolds, and I were packed into one of the small administrative offices.

"Well, then, please continue," Agent Loren said.

Dr. Reynolds cleared his throat. "From what Tempest has said, whenever he is injured, he still feels the pain. His bones still break, his skin still melts, his flesh is still torn, et cetera. His body then very, very quickly begins to heal itself. Regrowing skin, reattaching bones, you get the idea." Reynolds paused to collect his thoughts before continuing. "So, if we can somehow hit Richter with a large amount of heat and energy, we can cause his body to be totally destroyed before it has the chance to heal itself."

"You mean like hitting him with an explosive, like a missile?" Agent York asked.

Dr. Reynolds snapped his fingers in excitement. "Yes! Exactly."

York laughed and shook his head. "Have you done any research at all? We've tried hitting him with a missile. He either catches it, or it hits him and he walks it off."

"Yes, of course. But that's before we had Tempest," Reynolds said, giving a look of approval to me.

"What's your plan, exactly?" Agent Loren asked, clearly beginning to get perturbed with Reynolds.

"My plan," Reynolds began, "is that Tempest draws Richter out. The two of them fight, and Tempest leads Richter to a location far off in the desert. Tempest will keep Richter distracted and hopefully weaken him a bit. Then we launch a nuke at him. Tempest gets out of there right before it hits; Richter won't know what's coming, so he won't have time to deflect." Dr. Reynolds made the sound of an explosion, and a large gesture with his hands. "Boom. No more Richter. He's disintegrated, and his body has no chance of healing."

All of us mulled over Dr. Reynolds's plan. It sounded like it would work to me, although I was nervous about having to get Richter in the exact right spot for the nuke to hit him. I'd cross that bridge when I came to it, though.

"It sounds simple enough," Agent Loren said. "I like it."

Agent York nodded. "I agree. Sometimes the simplest plans are the best."

"Yeah, kinda amazing how you didn't think of this before."

"Oh, we did," Dr. Reynolds said. "But with every missile we sent his way, he would always deflect it before it got to him. We couldn't risk him catching it in the air and sending it toward an occupied city. Especially one in another country. Even if it was Richter's fault, it would most likely still cause an international incident and might lead to war, especially if he sent it to Pyongyang. We were hoping for a more elegant solution, but I believe this one will be the most success-ful. With you distracting him, he won't see the nuke coming at all."

I didn't like being reduced to bait, but I guessed it was, in a way, what I'd always thought they were using me for to begin with. Besides, if it led to the defeat of Richter, I was down for pretty much anything.

"It sounds to me like we have a plan," Agent York said.

Agent Loren nodded. "Indeed. I'll go make the necessary calls to get the warheads ready."

They were about to leave the room, but I stopped them. "What should I do?"

Dr. Reynolds replied, "We'll send a message to Richter. A message he can't refuse."

*

I stood in the parking lot of the middle school, with the destroyed gym of the high school in the background. A man who worked for Homeland Security stood a few feet away from me, holding a large news camera. Another stood next to him, pointing a microphone at me.

Everything felt so weird. I felt as if I was about to give a report on the weather, not like I was about to challenge a supervillain to a fight that would end in a nuclear explosion.

"We're ready whenever you are," the cameraman said.

I took a deep breath and looked into the camera, my eyes glowing bright. "Richter," I began in my altered voice. It sounded deeper than my normal voice, and slightly robotic. "I'll play your game. Let's begin round one on the mountaintop."

I stopped and said no more. That was all I needed. Richter

needed no convincing for a fight. He would know what I meant by the mountaintop. Yes, it was in Washington, far away from the Arizona desert where the nuke would go off, but I had to pick a location that wasn't suspicious. If I said, *Hey, meet me in the desert where they used to test nukes all the time,* he'd probably realize something was up. There was no doubt in my mind that we would be able to fight our way to Arizona, where, hopefully, I'd help to end the greatest threat the world had ever faced.

CHAPTER 32

THE FIGHT BEGINS

STANDING ON THE destroyed mountaintop next to the giant hole in the ground caused by yours truly, I scanned the sky, searching for any sign of Richter. So far, nothing. I wasn't worried, though. It would only be a matter of time before Richter showed up, and our plan would begin to play out.

The trees far beneath me waved back and forth in the wind, and I could see the trench in the ground caused by my punching Richter as hard as I could last time we were up here. I smiled, remembering how good that had felt. I eagerly awaited the moment when I'd be able to do that again.

"Any sign of him?" I asked.

"Nothing yet," the voice of Agent York crackled through the earpiece I wore.

I sighed in frustration. This was taking longer than it should have.

Then someone slammed to the ground in front of me, sending cracks shooting across the earth where he'd landed. It was Richter, and he was ready to play.

"Got tired of playing hero, did ya?" Richter said with a smile. "Wanna see how the gods play?"

"Not quite, Richter."

Before he had a chance to respond, I uppercut him at super-speed, sending him flying into the air. I jumped up and grabbed him, then changed course and flew straight down the hole in the mountain. I slammed him into the ground, causing cracks to web out from the impact site and up the walls. Our glowing eyes illuminated the area, and I could see small rocks begin to fall. The mountain began to moan, and the hole began to collapse.

I threw Richter up as hard as I could out of the hole, and I flew out after him, the hole collapsing beneath me.

Once we were back out, I grabbed Richter and threw him down onto the mountain. I flew down to him, and was ready to continue my beating, but he'd recovered from the sudden surprise and subsequent beating. He was ready and angry.

When I bent over to pick him up and throw him again, he kicked me hard in the chest, sending me flying backwards, and I landed on my knees. I gasped for air; my ribs had been crushed and my lungs had collapsed. I felt them crack and move back into place, and I began to breathe again just in time for Richter to punch me in the chest again. He put all his anger and rage behind the punch, and I went flying backwards off the mountain.

I fell down into the woods at the foot of the mountain, slamming through trees and sending them crashing to the ground.

I slid to a stop just as Richter jumped off the mountain and landed a few yards away from me. I scrambled up off the ground as Richter ran to my side, ready to punch me again. I dodged it, and got in two good punches to his torso.

Anger and frustration boiled within me, and I used it as the power behind my punches.

Richter ran to a tree, pulled it from the ground, and before I realized what was happening, he swung it like a bat, and I was the baseball.

I went flying high into the air, above the trees. I stopped myself in midair and turned around to see Richter flying right at me.

I dodged out of the way, and he went soaring past me. I couldn't help but smile a little at how dumb he must've felt in that moment. I was the matador and he was the bull.

He turned around and flew back toward me, but I started flying too, except in the opposite direction. I flew slowly enough that Richter would be able to keep up. He was hot on my tail as I began to fly south. I got a little too cocky, though, and underestimated Richter's speed. He caught up to me in seconds. We were in Seattle when he grabbed me and threw me.

I tumbled through the air, unable to correct myself. I hit glass hard, and went flying through some sort of observation deck, right on through the building, taking out everything my body touched. I fell through the other side, and that was when I realized that what Richter had thrown me through was the Seattle Space Needle.

I slammed into the empty Seattle street. Water from pipes I'd broken spewed into the air and back down onto me. I pushed myself up off the ground, every inch of my body in pain. I looked up at the sky to see where Richter was, only to find that he'd torn the observation deck of the Space Needle off the pole, and had sent it hurtling toward me.

I ran out of the way, but he'd thrown it so fast and hard, it almost wasn't enough. It slammed into the ground behind me, sending buildings all around me tumbling down. The shock wave of the impact sent me flying forward into some abandoned cars.

I got up and looked behind me. The top of the Space Needle sat in a pile of rubble in the ground. Dirt and dust filled the air and covered everything around me. All of the buildings in the immediate vicinity had been totally destroyed.

I looked around for Richter and saw him standing on top of the rubble, an evil smile stretched across his dirty face.

"Isn't this fun?" he shouted at me with his arms raised. He took in all the damage and destruction he'd caused. "I don't know why I didn't do this sooner. It's so—" He disappeared in a blur as he ran straight at me. He stopped inches away from my face, before I had time to react. "Therapeutic."

He grabbed my Tempest outfit and launched into the air. I was ready this time, though, and with a shout, I slammed my arm down onto his wrist as hard as I could, causing it to break and him to let go of me. Richter let out a sharp wince in pain.

"You're right," I shouted as I flew to his side. I grabbed his shirt and punched him twice in the face, hard. "This *is* therapeutic."

I let go of him and began flying south again, Richter close on my tail. This time I made sure I was going fast enough that he wouldn't catch me again. I flew toward the Arizona desert, where the nuke would strike—and end Richter once and for all.

CHAPTER 33

DETONATION

I T WAS ONLY a matter of seconds before we reached the Arizona desert. I had to slow down in order to look for the small blinking light they'd placed in the sand that you could only see if you were looking for it. Unfortunately, that gave Richter the perfect opportunity to tackle me to the ground.

He slammed into me, and the two of us tumbled across the desert floor, head over heels.

I spat out a mouthful of sand and turned to look for Richter. He was picking himself up off the ground and spitting out sand just like I was.

I searched for the flashing light but couldn't see anything. I began to feel frantic. "Guys, I can't see the light," I said.

There was no response from Agent York in my earpiece.

"Gu—"

Richter slammed into me before I could finish my words.

He brought me down to the ground and got on top of me. He pummeled me as hard as he could. I tried to fight him off me, but he was pressing down hard on my arms.

"Tempest, this wasn't my decision. I'm sorry," I heard Agent York's voice say through my earpiece.

I couldn't process what he meant, since Richter bashing my face in was a little distracting. I pushed my arm straight down at my side and flew straight out from underneath Richter. His fist slammed into the ground, causing a large pillar of sand to fly into the air.

I shot myself a few hundred yards away from Richter, and it took him a moment to realize that I was no longer there.

"York, what do you mea—" Before I could finish, though, I realized exactly what he meant.

A blinding flash of light reached my eyes, followed by a deafening boom. I turned around and flew away as fast as I could. The heat on my back was unbearable, and I felt my suit beginning to melt away.

I got far enough away that I couldn't feel the heat anymore, and turned around to see a mushroom cloud a few miles away, where Richter and I had been just moments before.

It all clicked. That was why the government agents had been so open to working with me. They were going to kill two birds with one stone, and take out both Richter and me with one nuke.

Anger boiled within me. I couldn't believe the people I was risking so much to protect would use me and try to kill me like that.

I floated to the ground and watched as the mushroom cloud began to dissipate. It was strangely beautiful, and my knees became weak at the sheer power and ferocity of it.

A large wall of dust and sand reached me, and began to pelt me. I shielded my eyes and waited for the mini-sandstorm to pass. Once it did, I looked upon the destruction.

There was a large crater where the nuke had gone off. I flew high above and slightly to the side of the crater, and looked down. I searched for Richter, but he wasn't down there. That meant the plan might have worked. If Richter had been disintegrated, there wouldn't be a body to find.

A smile crept across my face as I began to realize what had happened. Richter had finally been defeated. I'd won.

My skin felt prickly and uncomfortable, probably from the amount of radiation that was bombarding my body. I figured it was time to get out of there, before the agents realized I'd survived.

I turned around and saw something that made me feel as if I'd been punched in the gut. A few hundred yards away, Richter lay face down in the sand. While he'd still gotten hit by the nuke, he must have realized what was happening a split second before the missile hit him, and had been able to get far enough away that the blast hadn't disintegrated him.

I flew to his side and rolled him over in the sand. Blood oozed from his mouth, nose, and eyes. His skin was almost completely melted away, but it slowly began to web around his body as his healing powers began the recovery process.

I didn't know what to do. Nuking Richter was the only thing that had made sense, and he had been able to escape even that. If they could hurry up and nuke him now, while he was unconscious and recovering from the first explosion, that'd be perfect. No more Richter for sure this time. But firing nukes wasn't like shooting bullets from a gun. By the time one was ready, Richter would be fully recovered, furious, and ready to destroy everything in sight. I was afraid of what would happen when he was healed. I knew it'd be unlike anything the world had ever seen.

Which meant I didn't have much time to figure out how I would kill Richter, once and for all.

My earpiece crackled and rang. I brought my hand up to it, the sudden noise not only frightening me, but causing me pain.

"Hello? Tempest? Tempest, do you copy?" a woman's voice said, one I didn't recognize. The voice sounded young and eager.

"Who's this?" I said, unsure of what was going on.

There was a whoop of joy at the other end of the line before the woman regained her composure. "Alright, Tempest. Listen to me closely. Preliminary imaging from our satellites shows that you and Richter are still alive and well. Homeland Security has another nuke on its way, and it will be there any second."

"What's going on?" I asked, still confused as hell. "Who are you?"

"Hey, Tempest. *Nuke headed your way.* That's a little more important right no—"

The line went dead.

I looked to the sky, and in the distance, I could see a nuclear missile headed right toward me, a few hundred yards away and closing fast.

I jumped into the air and began to fly away. *That was a close one,* I thought. Once I got far enough away, I turned around to see the explosion.

Only to see the nuke was just a few yards away from hitting me.

I almost didn't have time to dodge out of the way. I shot straight toward the ground, and my heart shot to my throat. I looked up and watched as the missile made a wide turn. It changed its course and came straight for me.

I took off running across the desert floor. I looked over

my shoulder and saw the nuke was following me, just a few feet off the ground. It kicked up large plumes of sand, as if the sand was water and the nuke was water skiing.

I ran faster and faster, but the nuke was always close behind, not changing its course, staying straight as an arrow.

I didn't know what to do, or why the nuke was locked on to me, not Richter.

The earpiece, I thought. It wasn't locked on to Richter, because he didn't have an earpiece given to him by the people shooting the missile. They knew we'd be in the same place, so they figured they could just have the missile locked on to me.

I reached inside the headgear of my suit as I ran, but before I could pull the earpiece out and throw it onto Richter as I ran past him, I realized Richter wasn't where I'd left him.

I felt as if I should look behind me, and as I did, I saw Richter grab the missile and begin to fly upwards, fighting the thrusters of the nuke to get it off course. His face strained and spit flew as he fought with all his might. Finally, he got it to go off course. He lifted it up, and with the missile thrusters combined with Richter's flying, they shot over my head.

I pulled the earpiece out and crushed it in my hand. I leaped into the air and began flying after Richter and the nuke. Richter was furious and wanted revenge. I had a feeling I knew exactly where he was going to take the nuke: Ebon, Indiana.

I flew up behind Richter and punched him hard in the side. He had such a tight grip on the missile, though, that he didn't let go. He and the missile went tumbling to the right. He corrected himself, and flew on to Indiana.

I flew up behind him and grabbed his legs. I began to fly in the opposite direction, slowing him and the missile down.

He fought hard against me. Technically, he was winning, because he and the missile weren't stopping for anything. Still, it slowed them down quite a bit, which gave me more time.

Richter kicked at me, but I didn't let go.

"Son of a bitch!" he shouted. He let go of the nuke and twisted around to punch me. I dodged his punch and gave him a hard right cross to the left side of his face. He went tumbling through the air, and I flew for the missile that was now flying straight forward, not locked on to anything.

I wrapped my arms around it and began to pull it upwards. I had to go easy, and couldn't fly straight up. We were both moving fast, and a nuclear missile isn't exactly as flexible as the human body.

I reached the apex of my loop, and the missile began to head back toward the desert. In the meantime, Richter had recovered, and he wasn't giving up that easily.

He grabbed my back, but I let go of the missile with my right hand and elbowed him hard in the face. Now I was only holding on to the missile with one hand, and both the missile and I began to spin uncontrollably in the air.

I tried to correct our course. I wrapped both arms around the missile and hugged it tight. I became extremely disoriented, and my trying to do course correction turned to me just holding on for dear life, praying I got my bearings before the nuke and I went slamming into something, causing it to explode.

I felt the missile slip out from beneath me, and I scrambled for it in a panic, trying to grab hold of any part of it. I'd lost it, though, and once I got out of my tailspin, I realized that Richter had taken it back from me and was now trying to turn it back around and head toward Ebon.

That was when he made his mistake.

The fuel in the missile suddenly ran out, and its thrusters stopped working. That meant that the missile was now a hunk of nuclear explosive metal, and was much easier to maneuver. Richter had been in the middle of a loop with the missile, and now, without the thrusters, was overcompensating.

The nuke hurtled toward the ground, and Richter didn't have time to stop it.

I turned and flew as fast as I could, feeling the heat of a nuclear explosion on my back for the second time that day.

CHAPTER 34

PLAN B

I FELL INTO THE desert floor, having barely gotten away from the blast in time. I lay on the ground, heaving huge breaths as I stared up at the sky with the intense heat of the sun bearing down on me.

A few moments later, the sandstorm caused by the explosion began to pelt me. In a matter of seconds, it washed over me, but it was over almost as quickly as it had begun.

I stood, out of breath and tired. I brushed some of the sand off me and shook it out of my hair.

I scanned the area and saw a familiar body lying a good distance away from ground zero. I ran to it, and my fears were confirmed. It was Richter.

My mind crackled and began to ring. The loud sound echoed throughout my head, and I fell to my knees, clutching my ears, trying to get the sound to stop.

"Hello? Can you hear me?" a voice said in my head. It was the same woman as earlier.

My heart skipped a beat. "How are you doing this?" I asked. "I don't have the earpiece anymore."

The woman scoffed. "Listen, buddy, you and Richter aren't

the only ones with powers. Some of us aren't as public with them as the two of you are. But that's not the point. The point is, you need to get Richter into space, and fast. Without oxygen his body will take longer to heal. He still will, of course, but that will give us more time."

"More time for what?" I asked.

"To figure out how to kill him. Just grab him and get into space. Now!"

I didn't like taking orders from a voice inside my head, but she did have a good point.

I picked Richter's burned and battered body up and began to fly into the air. I flew straight up as fast as I could, reaching heights faster than I ever had before.

I didn't know who this woman was, talking inside my head, but the fact that she had superpowers worried me. Would I have to deal with another Richter as soon as I'd taken out the last one? The thought troubled me, but I pushed it out of my mind. *One thing at a time,* I told myself.

I reached low orbit and felt the terrifying sensation of not being able to breathe. It caught me off guard, and I faltered for a moment. I forced myself to stay calm, though, and pushed myself to fly even higher. With the low gravity and no wind resistance, I found myself shooting completely out of Earth's atmosphere and into space.

I began to feel claustrophobic, of all things. Like when I would go SCUBA diving, and I could see nothing but water in all four directions. Being in something so vast and infinite terrified me, and I felt helpless.

I did my best to push those feelings out of my mind. I had to focus on one thing, and one thing only: defeating Richter.

I wanted to talk to the woman, but I couldn't, up here

where there was no air to carry the sound of my voice. Then a thought occurred to me. Was she communicating telepathically?

"Hello?" I thought, unsure if the woman could hear me.

"Yes, hi," the woman said, crystal clear in my head. "Look this is what I've got. You need something hot and powerful to destroy Richter before his body can regenerate. There's nothing here on Earth that has enough energy to destroy all the power in his body."

"I can't just throw him into a volcano or something?" I thought. Man, that felt weird.

The woman laughed. "No, no, Tempest. That won't work. It's not powerful enough. The power inside of him will still be able to keep him alive."

I didn't follow, but she sounded like she knew a lot more about this stuff than I did, and she seemed like she was really trying to help. "So what do I do?" I asked. I looked down at Richter's body in my arms. His skin was very slowly piecing itself back together, and it was only a matter of time before he regained consciousness.

"Okay, this might be a little scary, and very risky. But the only thing really powerful enough is the Sun."

My stomach twisted in knots, and if I had been breathing, the breath definitely would have been knocked out of me. "The *Sun*?! That's ninety-three million miles away."

"And you can fly at super-speed, faster than any ship man has ever built. Without wind resistance, in zero gravity, you'll be able to fly at unheard of speeds. Maybe even close to the speed of light. When you get close to the Sun, its gravity should begin to pull you in as well, bringing you toward it even faster."

I gritted my teeth. This all actually sounded possible, but also terrifying. "This is my only option?"

"As far as I can tell, yes."

"Okay. I'll do it."

I heard a sigh of relief. "Okay, great. You'd better get a move on before Richter comes to. When you get back, I'll find you."

I felt as if a presence was beginning to leave my mind. "Wait!" I thought hard, hoping it would stop her. "What's your name?"

There was silence, and I thought I'd been too late. "Samantha," she said. "Now get Richter out of here. When you get back, I'll tell you everything."

Samantha left my mind, and I turned toward the bright, burning ball of fire ninety-three million miles away. I flew toward it, faster than I had ever flown before.

CHAPTER 35

FLIGHT

THE SPEED AT which I traveled terrified me. I held on tight to Richter's comatose body as the infinite blackness flew past me. Each second that went by, I traveled thousands of miles. Traveling at speeds this fast would be impossible on Earth, and I would surely slam into a building, or something else equally catastrophic, if I tried. So even though I was terrified by how fast I flew, it was kinda nice to "stretch my legs" in a way. I flew as fast as I could, and didn't have to worry about having to stop anytime soon, or crashing into something, or having anyone see me.

A huge sphere zipped by me so fast that if I'd blinked, I would have missed it. *Holy shit,* I thought. *I think I just flew by Venus.* I couldn't help but smile. *I just saw Venus.* That was the closest anyone had ever gotten to the planet named after the Roman goddess of love. I got so distracted thinking about it, enamored by its beauty and majesty, that I felt myself begin to slow down. I forced myself to stop thinking about it and pushed myself to fly even faster. Now was not the time to get distracted.

The Sun grew larger and larger as I got closer and closer. A few minutes passed by, then twenty, then thirty, then finally an hour. I was getting close to the Sun, but I still felt as if I was a long ways away.

I looked down at Richter and saw that his skin was almost completely done patching itself up. He'd be waking up anytime now.

I pushed myself to fly faster and faster. I felt I was going so fast I might explode.

The Sun got closer and closer, larger and larger. I was almost there. It was almost time to rid the universe of Richter once and for all.

I felt myself begin to go even faster, and it felt like someone was trying to pull me. It was the Sun's gravitational pull, dragging me in. I gave in to it, and in the blink of an eye, I found myself closer to the Sun than any man had ever been before—and might ever be. My body worked hard to replace the pieces of me that were melting before it was too late, but I knew I had to get out of there soon. My entire body felt weak from lack of oxygen, and from all the energy I had used flying so far so fast.

I took one last look at Richter. His skin was healed, and I could see his eyes beginning to move underneath their lids. It was now or never. "I won," I whispered as I pulled my arm back, then threw Richter toward the Sun as hard as I could.

One second he was there, the next, he was gone. The Sun pulled him in, welcomed him into her arms, and then devoured him, killing him once and for all.

I didn't have time for celebration. I had to get out of there fast. I turned around and began flying away. I felt the Sun tugging at me, not wanting me to leave. I could defy Earth's gravity easily, but the Sun was massive and its gravity was so much stronger than Earth's. I found it difficult to fight, especially in my weakened state. Still, I wouldn't give up. I pressed on as hard as I could, and like a rubber band stretched too far, once I broke free of the Sun's grasp, I launched into space, flying far, far away.

CHAPTER 36

ASLEEP AT THE WHEEL

I WANTED TO STOP and admire the planets as they zoomed by me, but my whole body felt weak and I craved oxygen. I couldn't afford to stop. Flying so fast had taken a lot out of me, as had my body constantly regenerating itself to keep me from turning into a melted blob when I was close to the Sun.

My eyes grew heavy, and I forced them to stay open. No way I'd fall asleep at the wheel. I had to get back to Earth, and fast. I didn't know what would happen if I passed out in space, but I knew it wouldn't be good. I needed oxygen for energy to return, and for my body to go back to normal. If it didn't, and I lost consciousness while hurtling through space, I might not wake up.

I saw a familiar blue planet far off in the distance, and I felt warmth well up inside me. I was almost home. I felt my body begin to slow down, not wanting to overshoot the planet. Once it did, though, a wave of weakness washed over me. My whole body felt as if it was going to shut down. My eyes grew heavy, and this time, I really had to fight to keep them open.

I opened them just in time to see the Moon come zooming up to meet me.

I slammed into its rocky surface hard and skidded across the ground, sending a plume of lunar soil shooting out in every direction. I rolled over onto my back and gasped for air, but there was none. I couldn't move. My body felt weak and screamed for air. I looked out at the Earth. All the air I would ever need was right there in front of me, but I couldn't find the strength to stand. I felt paralyzed. All the energy left in my body was being used to keep me alive.

I wanted to scream and yell and curse everything, but I couldn't. All I could do was look upon the Earth as it spun around peacefully in front of me, oblivious to the fact that its savior was fighting to stay alive on its Moon.

I took one last good look at Earth—at home. I gave up trying to get up; I simply didn't have the energy to fight. I took comfort and solace knowing that the Earth was safe from Richter. I'd done my job. I'd saved my family, my friends, my people. My work was done.

My eyes closed, and this time, I didn't try to fight them.

CHAPTER 37

BORN FOR THE GRAVE

September 19th, 2078

MRS. ANDREWS LOOKED at the clock and realized how late at night it was. She'd talked well into the late afternoon, and had to do a bit of cleaning before she retired for the night. "I'm sorry," she told Mr. Renner. "But that's all the time I have. That's the end of this story, anyway. I hope you've enjoyed yourself."

Leopold Renner looked at her, his eyes wide and filled with glee. "Oh, yes, of course, ma'am. I've had a wonderful time. Hearing Tempest's story told from his perspective like that was incredible for me personally. I've always been fascinated by the Supers, and this is going to make one hell of a story. With this piece, Tempest will be in the spotlight once again, I guarantee it."

Mrs. Andrews stood, as did Leopold. She shook his hand and gave him a warm smile. "Thank you, Mr. Renner. Kane would be so proud that the whole story is being told."

Leopold nodded. "I can't wait to get everything together." He knocked on the tablet in his hand. "I've got everything recorded right here. It'll take a few more weeks for me to gather all the information I need, but once my piece of Tempest and the Supers has been published, I'll make sure you get the first copy."

"I'd like that," Mrs. Andrews said as the two of them walked to the front door. She opened the door for him, and Leopold stepped out. "If you have any more questions, feel free to call me. I want to make sure you have everything you need."

"Yes, of course," Leopold said.

"I have many more stories to tell as well. If you ever find that you need inspiration, stop by any time. I'd love to sit with you and speak more about Kane if you'd like."

Leopold smiled. "I'd like that as well, Mrs. Andrews. You have a nice day," he said as he turned and walked down the steps of the front porch.

Mrs. Andrews stood at the front door and watched until Leopold had driven away. Once he was out of sight, she shut the door behind her.

She walked through the museum, past the many artifacts that Tempest had gathered through his Super days, to the back portion of the house where she lived. She walked into the bathroom and looked in the mirror.

She reached behind her ears and pulled two small silver devices from behind them. Suddenly, her reflection in the mirror changed. She was no longer a frail old woman, but instead, a beautiful young lady. She pulled her black hair out of the net it was in, and using a band she grabbed from one of the drawers, pulled her hair pack into a ponytail. She stripped out of her old dress and stockings and put on a black V-neck T-shirt.

She then opened one of the bathroom drawers and pulled

out a black and silver earbud. She placed it in her right ear, then clicked it on. "Call headquarters," she said. She realized she still had the voice changer on, so she still sounded like an old lady. She tapped her throat and felt a click as the voice changer embedded into her neck turned off.

Connecting to headquarters, the voice in her ear said.

"Verify," a man's voice at the other end of the line said moments later, coming through her earpiece crystal clear.

"Agent Cassidy, identification code seven seven Charlie Alpha Omaha five two."

"Okay, identity confirmed. How did it go today, Agent Cassidy?" the man asked.

"I did everything I was told. I told Leopold Renner everything that happened between Tempest and Richter, verbatim from what we gathered from Tempest's memory banks."

"Good. And Mr. Renner is going to the press with the story?"

"Yes. He seemed very eager," Cassidy said. She looked at her reflection in the mirror and fixed her eyebrows.

"Excellent work, Agent Cassidy. It seems everything is going according to plan."

"How'd Agent Damien's mission go?" she asked, her heart fluttering at the mention of his name.

"Agent Cassidy," the man growled. "Stay focused on your mission. We are entering phase two and cannot have any distractions. We only get one shot at this, and I will not have your personal feelings screwing this up, do you hear?"

Cassidy cowered, ashamed and angry that'd she'd asked. "Yes sir, I understand."

"What were you born for?" the man asked.

Cassidy looked into the mirror, her green eyes staring

back at her. "I was born for the grave," she answered, the same answer she'd been giving since she was a young child. The phrase that had been forced into her and all her classmates.

"Exactly. Don't you forget that."

She sighed. "Before I go, you have protection for Leopold, right?"

"Don't worry. Leopold is the most important person in the world right now. We have our people surrounding his apartment. The Underground won't get to him tonight." The man paused before continuing. "Get some rest. You've done well today. Your time jump is at 1800 hours tomorrow. See you then."

The line went dead and Cassidy pulled the earpiece out. She put her hands down on the bathroom counter and breathed in and out. She was dedicated to the cause, more so than most people. She wanted nothing more than to see the plan of her masters carried out. Still, she couldn't help but fight the fleeting feeling in her mind that she'd just made a terrible mistake.

*

Leopold Renner pulled up to his apartment and got out at the curb. He sent his car to park and walked inside. He ignored the greetings from the doorman, and the one from the woman behind the front desk. His mind was focused on only one thing: getting to his apartment and continuing to work.

He couldn't believe the information he had on his tablet. It was a story that he'd always wanted to know, even if most of the population had forgotten about it. Who was the man behind Tempest's mask? Now he knew, and soon the rest of the world would know exactly who Kane Andrews was.

He got into the elevator and punched the holographic button for the seventh floor. He felt as if the elevator was moving in slow motion. When it finally opened its doors, he practically ran out, heading straight for his apartment. He scanned his thumbprint and the door opened.

"Welcome home, Leopold," the voice of Miranda, the computer software that ran his apartment, said as he walked in.

"Thank you, Miranda," he said. "Get some coffee brewing for me, please."

"Of course, Leopold."

Leopold set his tablet down on his desk and made an upward hand gesture, causing the holographic screen on his desk to spring to life.

"I want all articles mentioning Tempest and the Supers from the time of his last fight with Richter to a year later."

A flood of Internet and newspaper articles filled the screen. While they loaded, he got up and grabbed his cup of coffee. He returned to his desk and began skimming through the articles, looking for one to catch his eye. After a bit of searching, he found one that did. The headline read:

NO SIGN OF RICHTER OR TEMPEST SIX MONTHS AFTER DISAPPEARANCE. THREE MORE SUPERS EMERGE IN MEANTIME.

"Miranda, turn off all notifications. I don't want any interruptions, okay?" Leopold said.

"Yes, sir," she said. "Should I power down as well?"

"No," Leopold said. He grabbed his coffee mug and lifted it up a bit in the air. "I'll need you to keep these coming."

"Of course, sir."

Leopold took a sip of his coffee and settled into his chair. He had a long night of reading ahead of him.

About the Author

Logan Rutherford is a twenty year old author living in Los Angeles. He writes full time, and loves hearing from his readers. You can get in contact with him at the following places:

www.authorloganrutherford.com
@loganrutherford
facebook.com/loganwrites
authorloganrutherford@gmail.com

Thank you for reading.